D1528921

The Other Side

Marga Minco

THE OTHER SIDE

Translated from the Dutch by
Ruth Levitt

PETER OWEN / *London*
UNESCO Publishing / *Paris*

PETER OWEN PUBLISHERS
73 Kenway Road London SW5 0RE

Translated from the Dutch *De andere kant*
First published in Great Britain 1994
English translation © Ruth Levitt 1994

**UNESCO Collection of Representative Works
European Series**

Publication has been made possible with financial support
from, among others, the Foundation for the Production
and Translation of Dutch Literature

ISBN 0–7206–0908–9
ISBN UNESCO 92–3–102882–1

A catalogue record of this book is available from
the British Library

Printed and made in Great Britain

Contents

The Other Side

Trees

Ruth was woken by a strange sound, which must have come from somewhere below in the house. She raised her head and listened. It was as though someone were singing softly. She asked herself who it could be, and then it occurred to her that her grandfather had come to stay with them the day before and was now performing his morning prayers. She pushed the bedclothes aside, got out of bed and went downstairs in her bare feet. A yellowish light shone through the pane above the door. She heard her grandfather clearly now. He was singing. It was not joyful singing; it sounded rather mournful.

She opened the door cautiously. Her grandfather stood praying by the window. She crept over to the armchair on tiptoe and hid behind it. He could not have seen her because he was entirely absorbed in praying and stood with his face turned away from her. She stared at him silently. The fringes of his small prayer-shawl stuck out from his shirt, which was unbuttoned at the top. Sometimes he fingered the fringes and kissed them. On his left arm – he had rolled his sleeve up above his elbow – was the black leather prayer-strap. The arm was white and very hairy at the wrist. She saw a few brown spots in between the turns of the strap. She thought: Grandfather has an old arm. There was another prayer-strap round his head. As he turned to her side she could see the little house in the middle of his forehead. It was like a die without numbers, which stayed in place despite the movements the old man made.

When the praying was over he began to roll up the straps slowly and securely. She could see clearly where it had been on his arm, and a pink streak was left on his forehead. He tucked the fringes under his shirt and buttoned it up. It had no collar; his neck was wrinkled and thin. Ruth stayed behind the chair until he had left the room. At the breakfast-table she hardly recognized her grandfather as the man she had seen at prayer. He wore a collar, a black tie and a black waistcoat with a wide gold chain suspended from it. There were gold links in the stiff cuffs that protruded from the sleeves of his jacket. They sometimes tapped against the edge of his plate.

Only the skull-cap was still on the back of his head. Later he changed it for a black hat when they went for a walk.

In the park, he pointed out to her with his walking-stick the ducks and swans, plants and trees. They were on a narrow path and Ruth watched a brown duck waddling awkwardly across the grass. Her grandfather looked upwards.

'You ought to know them well.'

'The ducks?'

'No, I mean the trees.' He told her the names of the trees that stood there.

'Do you know them all?' asked Ruth.

'Yes, I love trees. They are our friends, don't forget that.' And while they walked slowly further along the narrow avenue he told her that in the Talmud it is written that it is not good to live in a town where there are no trees. 'Because a town without trees is not a real town.'

He stopped by a bench under a tree, propped his stick against the arm and unbuttoned his overcoat. He stretched his arms out wide and breathed deeply through his mouth, his head back a little. 'That's healthy,' he said, continuing to breathe deeply. 'You do it too.'

Ruth copied her grandfather.

'Do you feel how healthy it is?'

'Yes.' She couldn't feel anything but did not want to disappoint him.

'Come.' He laughed and buttoned up his coat. 'We've done something healthy again. Now we can prepare ourselves better for tomorrow. You know what day it is tomorrow, of course?'

'Yes. The fifteenth of Shevat.'

'Exactly. The New Year of Trees.'

At home Miss Kagel had come to visit her mother. She was going round the community with little bags of almonds from Palestine. She also had a red earthenware pot with a thin plant in it.

'This is a cutting of a tree,' said Miss Kagel.

'That's nice,' said her grandfather. 'I shall give it to Ruth for the fifteenth of Shevat.' He recited a Hebrew text that she did not understand.

'Will it turn into a tree?' asked Ruth. She took the pot in her hands.

There was only a small green stalk in the earth. It could just as well have become a flower – a rose or a violet.

'A proper tree,' said her mother.

She took the little plant to her room, put it on a small table and sat on the edge of her bed looking at it. She wanted to take good care of it. Now every day she would see how the cutting was growing. Slowly it would become a tree, a trunk with branches and leaves. A tree in her room, under which she could lie down when she was tired, which she could dance round when she was happy and lean against when she was sad. One day it would push through the ceiling and then through the roof, its crown above the house. And everyone would know that it was her tree. She felt that she need never again be frightened. The tree would protect her from everything.

But the cutting did not become a tree. Not because it was impossible in such a small pot. They could always have replanted it in larger pots and later put it out in the garden. The cutting had hardly sprouted before they had to leave their house. Not long after that her parents as well as her grandfather were carried off. Ruth ended up with a family in a village. There were so many trees there that she didn't think about an 'own' tree any more. She no longer knew when the New Year of Trees was, the almonds day, the nuts and fruits on the table laid for celebration. And there was no one around to remind her.

Shortly after the Liberation she returned to the town. Her parents and her grandfather did not return. She walked along the street where she had lived. On the opposite side she stood looking at the house. There were strange curtains in the windows. The top window had been her room. On the frames she had pinned the postcards members of the family always sent her. It seemed that the windows were smaller than she recalled. She had also never noticed that the step in front of the house had slipped crookedly. She crossed the road. There was someone in the room, a man; he was folding a newspaper open. A boy came outside and slammed the front door behind him. It had been dark in the passage, she couldn't see anything there. She went on through the old neighbourhood; so much had changed; it seemed as though she had lived there a lifetime ago.

Much later she remembered the cutting she had once received from her grandfather. He had taught her the names of the trees in the park, explained to her how much they meant to people and to the places where they lived. She knew again how, together under the leaves, with mouths open wide and outstretched arms, they had breathed in the pure air.

Now she would plant trees for him and for her parents in the Forest of Martyrs; three trees, which would bear their names for ever. There they will find each other again when the wind entwines their branches as their leaves touch and caress each other and rejoice for rains of the season and the cool of each other's shadow.

And every year their crowns will grow wider and reach higher into the sky.

The Address

'Do you still know me?' I asked.

The woman looked at me searchingly. She had opened the door a chink. I came closer and stood on the step.

'No, I don't know you.'

'I'm Mrs S's daughter.'

She held her hand on the door as though she wanted to prevent it opening any further. Her face gave absolutely no sign of recognition. She kept staring at me in silence.

Perhaps I was mistaken, I thought, perhaps it isn't her. I had seen her only once, fleetingly, and that was years ago. It was most probable that I had rung the wrong bell. The woman let go of the door and stepped to the side. She was wearing my mother's green knitted cardigan. The wooden buttons were rather pale from washing. She saw that I was looking at the cardigan and half hid herself again behind the door. But I knew now that I was right.

'Well, you knew my mother?' I asked.

'Have you come back?' said the woman. 'I thought that no one had come back.'

'Only me.'

A door opened and closed in the passage behind her. A musty smell emerged.

'I regret I cannot do anything for you.'

'I've come here specially on the train. I wanted to talk to you for a moment.'

'It is not convenient for me now,' said the woman. 'I can't see you. Another time.'

She nodded and cautiously closed the door as though no one inside the house should be disturbed.

I stood where I was on the step. The curtain in front of the bay window moved. Someone stared at me and would then have asked what I wanted. 'Oh, nothing,' the woman would have said. 'It was nothing.'

I looked at the name-plate again. *Dorling* it said, in black letters on white enamel. And on the jamb, a bit higher, the number. *Number 46.*

As I walked slowly back to the station I thought about my mother, who had given me the address years ago. It had been in the first half of the war. I was home for a few days and it struck me immediately that something or other about the rooms had changed. I missed various things. My mother was surprised I should have noticed so quickly. Then she told me about Mrs Dorling. I had never heard of her but apparently she was an old acquaintance of my mother, whom she hadn't seen for years. She had suddenly turned up and renewed their contact. Since then she had come regularly.

'Every time she leaves here she takes something home with her,' said my mother. 'She took all the table silver in one go. And then the antique plates that hung there. She had trouble lugging those large vases, and I'm worried she got a crick in her back from the crockery.' My mother shook her head pityingly. 'I would never have dared ask her. She suggested it to me herself. She even insisted. She wanted to save all my nice things. If we have to leave here we shall lose everything, she says.'

'Have you agreed with her that she should keep everything?' I asked.

'As if that's necessary,' my mother cried. 'It would simply be an insult to talk like that. And think about the risk she's running, each time she goes out of our door with a full suitcase or bag.'

My mother seemed to notice that I was not entirely convinced. She looked at me reprovingly and after that we spoke no more about it.

Meanwhile I had arrived at the station without having paid much attention to things on the way. I was walking in familiar places again for the first time since the war, but I did not want to go further than was necessary. I didn't want to upset myself with the sight of streets and houses full of memories from a precious time.

In the train back I saw Mrs Dorling in front of me again as I had the first time I met her. It was the morning after the day my mother had told me about her. I had got up late and, coming downstairs, I saw my mother about to see someone out. A woman with a broad back.

'There is my daughter,' said my mother. She beckoned to me.

The woman nodded and picked up the suitcase under the coat-rack. She wore a brown coat and a shapeless hat.

'Does she live far away?' I asked, seeing the difficulty she had going out of the house with the heavy case.

'In Marconi Street,' said my mother. 'Number 46. Remember that.'

I had remembered it. But I had waited a long time to go there. Initially after the Liberation I was absolutely not interested in all that stored stuff, and naturally I was also rather afraid of it. Afraid of being confronted with things that had belonged to a connection that no longer existed; which were hidden away in cupboards and boxes and waiting in vain until they were put back in their place again; which had endured all those years because they were 'things'.

But gradually everything became more normal again. Bread was getting to be a lighter colour, there was a bed you could sleep in unthreatened, a room with a view you were more used to glancing at each day. And one day I noticed I was curious about all the possessions that must still be at that address. I wanted to see them, touch, re-member.

After my first visit in vain to Mrs Dorling's house I decided to try a second time. Now a girl of about fifteen opened the door to me. I asked her if her mother was at home.

'No,' she said, 'my mother's doing an errand.'

'No matter,' I said, 'I'll wait for her.'

I followed the girl along the passage. An old-fashioned iron Hanuk-kah candle-holder hung next to a mirror. We never used it because it was much more cumbersome than a single candlestick.

'Won't you sit down?' asked the girl. She held open the door of the living-room and I went inside past her. I stopped, horrified. I was in a room I knew and did not know. I found myself in the midst of things I did want to see again but which oppressed me in the strange atmos-phere. Or because of the tasteless way everything was arranged, because of the ugly furniture or the muggy smell that hung there, I don't know; but I scarcely dared to look around me. The girl moved a chair. I sat down and stared at the woollen table-cloth. I rubbed it. My fingers grew warm from rubbing. I followed the lines of the pattern. Somewhere on the edge there should be a burn mark that had never been repaired.

'My mother'll be back soon,' said the girl. 'I've already made tea for her. Will you have a cup?'

'Thank you.'

I looked up. The girl put cups ready on the tea-table. She had a broad back. Just like her mother. She poured tea from a white pot. All it had was a gold border on the lid, I remembered. She opened a box and took some spoons out.

'That's a nice box.' I heard my own voice. It was a strange voice. As though each sound was different in this room.

'Oh, you know about them?' She had turned round and brought me my tea. She laughed. 'My mother says it is antique. We've got lots more.' She pointed round the room. 'See for yourself.'

I had no need to follow her hand. I knew which things she meant. I just looked at the still life over the tea-table. As a child I had always fancied the apple on the pewter plate.

'We use it for everything,' she said. 'Once we even ate off the plates hanging there on the wall. I wanted to so much. But it wasn't anything special.'

I had found the burn mark on the table-cloth. The girl looked questioningly at me.

'Yes,' I said, 'you get so used to touching all these lovely things in the house, you hardly look at them any more. You only notice when something is missing, because it has to be repaired or because you have lent it, for example.'

Again I heard the unnatural sound of my voice and I went on: 'I remember my mother once asked me if I would help her polish the silver. It was a very long time ago and I was probably bored that day or perhaps I had to stay at home because I was ill, as she had never asked me before. I asked her which silver she meant and she replied, surprised, that it was the spoons, forks and knives, of course. And that was the strange thing, I didn't know the cutlery we ate off every day was silver.'

The girl laughed again.

'I bet you don't know it is either.' I looked intently at her.

'What we eat with?' she asked.

'Well, do you know?'

She hesitated. She walked to the sideboard and wanted to open a drawer. 'I'll look. It's in here.'

I jumped up. 'I was forgetting the time. I must catch my train.'

She had her hand on the drawer. 'Don't you want to wait for my mother?'

'No. I must go.' I walked to the door. The girl pulled the drawer open. 'I can find my own way.'

As I walked down the passage I heard the jingling of spoons and forks.

At the corner of the road I looked up at the name-plate. *Marconi Street*, it said. I had been at Number 46. The address was correct. But now I didn't want to remember it any more. I wouldn't go back there because the objects that are linked in your memory with the familiar life of former times instantly lose their value when, severed from them, you see them again in strange surroundings. And what should I have done with them in a small rented room where the shreds of black-out paper still hung along the windows and no more than a handful of cutlery fitted in the narrow table drawer?

I resolved to forget the address. Of all the things I had to forget, that would be the easiest.

Something Different

'Why did you do it?' asked the man. He sat behind a small desk and adjusted the paper in his typewriter. She gazed at his hair, which was carefully combed back, and at his ears, which stood out a little. He kept his fingers on the keys and looked at her.

'I don't know.'

She sat opposite him, her hands clasping her bag. Behind the man's head was a map of Amsterdam with here and there red circles across it.

'Have you ever done this before?' he asked, not unkindly.

'Never.'

'Think about it carefully.' He observed her closely.

He's quite a bit younger than me, she thought.

'It's really true.'

She let go of her bag and played with a coat button. At a table in the other corner of the room there was a red-faced man in his shirt-sleeves, his tie loose. He was eating a split herring with a fork on a newspaper on the blotter in front of him. With his left hand he carefully picked the bones out of the herring and smeared them on to the paper. One bone remained on his finger. It protruded like a stubborn hair.

'Did you plan to do it?'

'No.'

'What does your husband do?'

'He's on the board of directors at an engineering factory.'

'So he's got a good job.'

'Oh yes. He handles all the exports. He often goes abroad.'

'And you go with him, then?'

'No. I never go when my husband has business trips.'

'What will he say about this?'

'I don't know,' she said hesitantly. Jules will never know about it, she thought. He never notices anything. He hardly knows what I'm like. He wouldn't believe it if they told him. I needn't worry on that score.

She smelt the sickly smell of the herring. The man had now eaten half of it. He scraped the skin and licked the greasy fork. The bone still stuck to his finger.

'Perhaps your husband would tell me why you did it?'

She shrugged her shoulders. 'I don't think so.'

'Or do you know now?' He put a hand on the keyboard. Some of the letters were pressed down and stood up in front of the ribbon.

'Oh, it just happened.' She put the button through the buttonhole and back again. 'I've never done anything like it before. You read about it now and then in the paper. Women whom you wouldn't expect to get caught. Occasionally I wondered how those women felt, what they went through at that moment.'

She sighed and continued softly, as though she spoke only for herself. 'Everything is so alike. Each day is the same.'

'Do you have children?'

'No.' She undid the button. 'You just want something different once . . . it doesn't matter what, as long as it's different.'

'So you did plan to do it,' he said.

'No. I decided on the spur of the moment. I'd really never thought of it before.'

He typed some more.

How did I actually decide to do it? she thought. Each afternoon she went into town and came home exhausted. They were always the same shops, she always looked at the same things. Sometimes she bought something even if she didn't need it. She had gone into a large clothes shop, a bargain store, not deliberately. Women jostled each other in front of long racks and searched eagerly through the clothing. She was pushed aside and ended up standing beside a rack of pullovers. She took a green one and someone showed her the changing-room, a narrow passage that led to small cubicles closed by curtains. It was reminiscent of a swimming-pool, and it also smelt rather steamy. In the cubicle there was scarcely room to take one step backwards. She held up the pullover. I'm going to put it on, she thought, since I'm here now.

She looked in the mirror as she took off her coat and unbuttoned her blouse. Her face was red, her lower lip trembled. All of a sudden she thought of André. He was a foreign business acquaintance of her husband's, with whom she had had a brief affair during his stay in town.

The same mirror had hung in his hotel room. When she stood in front of it he always came up behind her and, with his arms around her, unbuttoned her blouse. I was much thinner then, she thought. She put her hands beneath her bra and pulled her stomach in. Jules never found out about it. She felt a strange nervousness, her hands shook and she could not find the pullover's arm-holes, her ring caught in the woollen fabric. She jerked at it, a thread snagged. Hastily she pulled the sweater over her head. She put the hanger on the chair but her coat was there and the hanger fell to the floor. She bent over, picked it up, pushed it behind the mirror and put her blouse on. The pullover prickled her skin; she felt hot, as though she were standing in the blazing sun. I can never give the pullover back, I'm sweating all over, I must keep calm, no one must notice anything about me. She combed her hair, put her coat on and drew the curtain aside. Women were waiting there with clothes over their arms. One of them pushed past behind her to get into the cubicle and quickly drew the curtain again.

'Should I take this?' someone called.

Slowly she went out of the changing-room. In the shop it had become even busier. A female voice called out a number over the loudspeaker. A cash till bell rang. A young male shop assistant came straight up towards her. She stopped for a moment, but he was looking for someone behind her. She felt a violent itching in her armpits and over her stomach. At the exit a fat man stood with his hands behind his back. He looked at her. The doorman opened the door for her. A woman rushing in collided with her. 'Sorry,' she said. The woman passed in silence. It's perfectly simple, just a few more steps then I turn into a side-street. Her legs trembled, it was as though she had to force herself to continue. Two girls were pointing out something in the window to each other. She felt a hand on her shoulder.

'Have you been into that shop before?' asked the detective.

She looked up. 'No, I always shop at other places.'

'Would you have shown that jumper to your husband if you had taken it home?'

She shrugged her shoulders. 'He doesn't pay any attention to such things.' Jules never sees if I've got anything new on. It doesn't interest him.

'If you hadn't been arrested, would you have taken the jumper home without paying for it?'

'Yes.' She felt the hand on her shoulder again. Before she turned round she saw a man on the opposite side with a fruit barrow coming out of an alley. He shouted something. The woman behind her had been walking fast. Out of breath, she asked her to accompany her.

'Why?'

'A sweater's missing,' said the shop assistant.

The doorman held the door open for them. The fat man still stood in the same spot. Women looked at her and turned towards her. I must make something up. I can't let this happen. Again she felt the pullover prickling all over her body; it seemed as though it covered her down to her knees. She was left in a kind of store-room where a man in an overall was lugging crates and boxes.

'Take off your coat.'

A second saleswoman arrived in a black skirt with pins on her front. She let them undo the top button of her blouse. The women looked at her as though they had discovered she had a virulent rash.

'Have you been involved with the police before?' asked the detective.

'No, never.'

Another man was busy filling an old whistling kettle at a small sink. He put it on a gas ring, rinsed out a coffee-pot and put coffee into it from a canister. He carefully swept up the coffee he had spilt next to it with one hand into the other.

Someone came in, leaving the door wide open. 'My scooter's been stolen,' he cried angrily.

'Wait in the corridor,' said the detective. 'You can see I'm busy.'

'You can't trust anyone any more,' shouted the other. He slammed the door behind him. She heard him stamping heavily on the wooden floor.

'He's right,' said the man by the sink. He looked at a small cracked mirror above the tap and pulled his mouth into a strange grimace.

'So that's what happened.' The detective studied the sheet full of typing.

It was a long time since anything had happened. Again she thought of André. He had lived in a small hotel for a few months. She went to him every afternoon. She remembered how uneasy she was before she went and how excited she felt when she came to the street where the hotel was. She walked much faster, but sometimes she hesitated slightly on the pavement in front of the revolving door. Each time the porter made her say whom she had come to see. He had a stony face. As she went up, she tapped the brass rods with the points of her shoes. When she went down, she pushed her heels deep into the carpet and looked at the mat at the bottom of the stairs, which had the hotel's name in upside-down letters. When André had gone, at first she had no idea what to do with her afternoons. So she went into town to shop. She never managed to think of anything else.

'Here,' said the detective, 'will you read through this and sign it?' He pulled the sheet out of the machine and put it in front of her.

She saw her name on it. A few words were crossed out with x's. She read one sentence, then another; the words swam into each other. She leant closer over the page and screwed her eyes up half closed. He gave her a pen.

'Do you agree with it?' he asked.

'Yes.' She signed.

'This statement goes to the public prosecutor now.' He opened a drawer and took out a folder.

The herring-eater had crumpled up the newspaper with the fish leftovers and thrown it in the bin. He started on a piece of brown bread and butter. The man at the sink put three mugs out ready.

'And then?' she asked.

'You may have to appear.'

He opened the folder and pointed to a door. 'Wait next door.'

Before the detective had questioned her she had taken the pullover off in a small room. The price-tag was still on it. She looked out of the window at a high blank wall. Could anyone get out of here? Now what did she have to wait for again? They had kept her waiting in the store-room a long time too. The man in the overall had watched her in silence all that time. The detective's arrival had been a relief.

'Will you come with me?' he asked in a friendly way, as though suggesting they should go for a cup of coffee.

They reached the street by a different door. Just like in a theatre, she thought, there's a separate exit for the actors.

'Where are we going?' she asked.

The man smiled. 'Look out,' he said, 'we're crossing over.' Two trams passed each other, cars drove bumper to bumper, cyclists weaved through skilfully. 'It's perilous here at this time of day, they drive recklessly and only think of themselves.' They crossed over. He put his hand on her arm as a car tried to pass in front of them. 'Out this side.'

They came to a narrow street with almost no traffic. Pedestrians walked in the road. Chinese lanterns and little flags hung outside a toy shop. Music came from several cafés. A boy on a delivery bike called something to a woman leaning out of a window. She was fat. Her heavy breasts rested on the window-sill. She laughed loudly.

'I've never been here,' she said.

'It's a red-light district.'

'That's precisely why. You have to be so careful. I'd rather stay away.'

'You're right,' he said. He pointed to a large open door. 'Here we are.'

'I didn't know that there was a police station here.'

'No?'

He let her go first. Two policemen stood in the corridor talking loudly to one another. Without their caps they looked less official than usual.

She leant against the edge of the table. In the other room someone was on the telephone. She tried to catch what was being said but couldn't understand a word. She didn't care. She was tired.

The door of the room opened. 'You may go,' said the detective. 'You'll be hearing further about it.'

In the corridor the man with the stolen scooter paced up and down impatiently. 'Is he ready?' he asked.

She nodded. Two young policemen came in laughing and moved aside to let her pass. She hurried along the street. There was a hurdy-gurdy at the end of it. A man rattled a brass cup under her nose; she shrank back and pushed it away. She stopped in the main street to hail a taxi. It was as though everyone was looking at her. A girl in a dark skirt watched her. I've been recognized, she thought. She started to feel hot again. All over her body she felt she was sweating, as though she still had the pullover on. She was glad a taxi arrived. With a sigh she slumped on the back seat.

'Tired from shopping, lady?' asked the driver.

She did not reply. She saw herself in the mirror above the windscreen: the powder on her face was caked and made the creases round her mouth appear more pronounced, a strand of grey hair fell on to her forehead, her eyelids were thick and puckered and smudged with mascara.

She stretched out her legs, kicked her shoes off. Her belt cut into her stomach; she leant back so that it bothered her less. The taxi took a sharp bend, causing her to hold on tight to the seat. She felt queasy from the petrol smell and undid the top button of her blouse. It was no longer very secure, she could pull it right off.

It's already almost seven years since I spent my afternoons in that hotel. She looked at her watch.

This afternoon is over, she thought.

The Drawing

Katie knocked her knee against the table-leg a few times. The milk in my mug is already shaking nicely, she thought, but not yet quite enough. She had a mind to kick out hard once with her foot, just to see how her father would shout, drop his newspaper on his plate into his fried egg. She did not do it; this morning she was reluctant to face the fuss that would ensue, the questions 'why', again and again, to which an ordinary 'because' never seemed sufficient. She had altogether different plans.

'Why don't you eat?' asked her mother.

'I'm not hungry.' It was not true; on the contrary she was as hungry as anything but she had decided not to eat; she wanted to sustain it as long as possible.

'Are you ill?' asked her mother.

'No, I'm not ill. I just don't feel like eating. Isn't that possible?'

'Then there must be something wrong with you. I'll ring the doctor immediately.'

'Who's ill?' asked her father. He let his paper drop without its touching his plate. He looked at Katie over his glasses.

'She's not eating,' said her mother. Her voice sounded tearful. 'Why doesn't she eat? It isn't normal. Something must be the matter.'

'I can't see anything,' said her father. 'She doesn't look ill at all. She must have eaten too many sweets yesterday. Tell me, how was it yesterday, actually?'

'She won't tell us anything about that either,' continued her mother in the same tone. 'I've already asked dozens of times. She doesn't understand that we're curious about it.'

'Go on, then,' Katie sighed. 'I'll eat something.'

'No, that's not what I'm asking you now,' said her mother. 'Surely, you can say whether it was nice or not?'

'Yes, that doesn't seem so difficult to me,' said her father.

'It was nice,' said Katie. She reached for the bread basket. She gave her mug a shove with her elbow.

'Was it nice? Oh! Watch what you're doing!' Her mother jumped up and went to the kitchen.

'I couldn't help it, I didn't see the mug there.'

The milk quickly spread over the table. She stopped the flow with her knife but couldn't prevent it running to the end of the table and exploding on the floor in little stars. Her father merely sat a bit further back, still reading his paper. Her mother returned with cloths.

'Look how beautifully I've held it back with my knife.'

'But it's running down on this side.' Her mother tried to catch the milk on two sides simultaneously. 'Ach, how awful. Just when it was a clean table-cloth too. Didn't you . . . ?'

'Oh, it's already late. I must go.' Katie picked up her school bag that lay next to her chair.

'You've still plenty of time.' Her mother knelt down and rubbed over the wet patch on the carpet. 'Why have you been going to school so early recently?'

'I've made arrangements with girl-friends, we discuss our home-work.'

She quickly put her coat on in the passage. Her mother's shawl fell on to the floor. She let it lie there.

In case they watched her through the bay window, at first she walked normally down the road. At the corner she began to run. She turned into a side-road and went on at a trot. Her bag knocked against her legs. Sometimes she slowed down in order to catch her breath. She noticed she had no pain from her empty stomach and even did a better time than the day before. People probably watched with surprise and children called 'Look at that fatty', but she ignored it. There was the prospect of soon being like other children, not fat any more; as long as she walked a lot every day and ate as little as possible.

She came to a neighbourhood she had never been in before. At that moment a tram stopped at a shelter. Everyone got out, including the driver and the conductors. The men went inside the shelter, took off their caps, wiped their brows and rolled cigarettes. She had grown hot from the brisk walking, her temples throbbed, she had shooting pains in her side. Perhaps she really was ill, then she wouldn't have to eat anything at all. She switched her bag to her other hand.

In front of a school children played leapfrog, a game she never took part in because she always had to stand. Often they kicked her dress on purpose and pushed her over. And if she said she didn't want to play, they called her a coward, fat coward. Cora was nice. She wondered whether she was still waiting for her. Actually she wasn't sure whether she found Cora nice. She had thought she was her friend and sometimes she walked home with her. But she never went in.

'She's my friend,' she had said to her mother.

'Ask her here, then,' said her mother, 'and I'll bake a cake.'

'Oh no,' she said. 'She always has to go straight home.'

One day Cora said: 'Your mother says that I am your friend.'

'Did my mother say that? When?' Curse it, she's interfering again.

'Yesterday she called to me when you had already gone in.'

'What do you care? My mother nags.'

'Do you know what I said?'

They were right by the school. Cora climbed up the fence.

'No,' said Katie. She saw a gang from the class in the playground.

'I said . . .' – Cora waited until she had first jumped down from the fence; she came up close to Katie and dug her in the back – 'I said: perhaps, perhaps not, I said to your mother.' The others stood watching at a distance. Cora walked over towards them. She turned back to Katie. 'You can come too.'

'Come where?'

'Wednesday afternoon. I'm having a birthday party.'

'Who else are you asking?'

'One or two from the class.' She ran off.

I'm not going, Katie thought. But she was almost certain that Guy would be there. And so she did go.

She slowed down a little for the last bit of the way to school. Otherwise she would look so sweaty. Tomorrow I'll make an even larger detour, she decided, it's becoming proper training. She hadn't seen Cora anywhere. Perhaps it was already later than she thought. Actually she ought to come in late once. Everyone would be surprised if she calmly walked into the class. If the teacher asked her why she was so late she would say: 'I didn't feel like coming on time today.' Then she would walk quietly to her place, without blushing or knocking against a desk. They would be amazed at her because she had spoken so decisively the teacher wouldn't know what to reply. A clock in a shop showed her there was still enough time. A group would be watching her at the corner. Now she walked very slowly.

If only she had stayed at home yesterday! She could feel herself colouring as soon as she went in. They stood round the table in paper hats and greeted her with jeers. Cora's mother didn't accompany her. 'Go straight in,' she said in the hall, 'everyone's there already.' She gave Cora her present and accepted a glass of lemonade.

'We're playing observatory,' they said to her. 'It's your turn.' She had to sit on a chair with a raincoat over her. 'Look up carefully through the sleeve,' someone said to her.

'I can't see anything,' she said. At that moment she felt water splashing into her face. She jumped up, terrified; the water ran down her neck; the collar of her dress was wet.

At hide-and-seek they hadn't made much of an effort to find her when she had hidden in a cupboard in the hall. After a very long time she crawled out again. The others had been playing something else for some time. So it went on the whole afternoon. Guy did not look at her once. Cora was elated, screeching as she walked through the house banging on the doors. 'We're going to play doctors,' she said.

If only she had left earlier! Now there was no more chance to do so. Guy was doctor. 'Katie is the patient,' cried one of the girls. 'Katie is ill.'

The table was cleared. Guy wore a white apron. 'Undress her,' he said. He tapped a spoon on the table.

She felt herself break out in a sweat all over. My dress is full of marks, she thought.

Guy took her hand in order to feel her pulse. 'She's got clammy hands,' he cried. He had a high, shrill voice. 'It will definitely need surgical intervention.'

They lifted her on to the table.

'First the anaesthetic,' said Guy.

They tied a wet rag over her nose and mouth. Someone pulled at the collar of her dress.

'Let's see,' said Guy.

'I don't want to,' she said. She heard something tearing. 'I don't want to,' she screamed.

It went quiet. Cora's mother came in and put a stop to the game. She stayed sitting on the table, she felt dizzy, her dress was ruined, her hair in a tangle.

She heard the bell in the distance. She walked back along the street and waited in front of a shop. It was a pâtisserie. She had often bought cream cakes there with her pocket-money; but recently had she given that up. They were standing in a line now, now they were going in the gate, now they were at the coat pegs. The second bell. Good that she was not there yet: the others would think she was ill from yesterday. A woman placed a tray of cakes in the shop window. They had red and green fruits on top. There were little pieces of pineapple in the whipped cream tarts. They had language for the first lesson. Cora was monitor that week, she had to hand round the exercise books. Would she put one on her desk? Someone had already gone inside the shop. She was surprised anyone would want to buy cakes so early. The woman chatted with the customer, she pointed to the child in front of the window. Katie walked on.

The square was empty. It seemed lighter than at other times. She thought about a coloured picture postcard her aunt had once sent her from Italy. It had a square with a terrace on one side. At the little tables there were men in light summer clothes, thin, bronzed women. Later on she too would go there, she would sit on a terrace in the sun.

Grumbling, the school keeper opened the door for her. It was quiet in the class. They sat bent over their work. When she came in they looked up and pulled faces at her. The teacher's voice was biting.

She said something, she stammered. She felt herself blush when she went to her place, she bumped into the front desk. Blindly she opened the exercise book in front of her.

It was hot in the class. Her legs tingled, she had the shooting pain in her side again and a mild cramp in her stomach. She heard the teacher continuing with the lesson. She noticed something going on between the children around her. The girls in front of her were repressing laughter. She saw notes going from hand to hand under the benches. She looked at Guy. He sat diagonally in front of her in the other row. He had blue-black hair and a brown complexion. His parents came from France but he spoke ordinary Dutch. He was slight and supple. His brown eyes strayed round the class continuously. When he laughed, only his mouth showed it. He often looked round, but then to the left or right of her or just through her. He never said hello if she encountered him in the street.

Perhaps it was because she was tired. The long journey through the town and the hunger had rather dazed her. Otherwise she would never have dared do such a thing. It was also because she thought something was brewing. She ascribed the suppressed giggles to something with a double meaning. I know exactly what's going on. They're keeping me out of it because they think I don't know anything about it. But I know exactly what's in the notes. I know much more than they do. I've found books in the bottom of my father's cupboard. She carefully tore a page out of her exercise book. I'll show them something for once. She drew a doll, a little naked man with wooden arms and legs and greatly enlarged genitals. Sweat droplets formed on her brow and nose. She folded the paper twice and passed it on. She saw it go along the rows. It was quickly looked at and then passed on again. Heads bent further over the benches. Sniggering could be heard. She received the note back at the very moment the teacher discovered the disruption. Quikly she hid it in her desk. The teacher was already standing next to her.

The square was deserted again when she crossed it. The covered cycle-rack was empty. It seemed like a small terrace whose chairs had been removed. She thought she would be expelled from the school when the head and the teacher had taken her in; she had hoped so. At a different school they don't know anything about you, a new child is always at the centre of things, all the girls want to be friends with you. But perhaps they would be different to her tomorrow. They'd noticed now that she too dared to do something. Guy would certainly look at her now, perhaps talk to her.

It didn't bother her that they were waiting for her in the porch. She saw them only when she had almost gone past them. She wanted to stop where she was.

'Coward,' they called. 'Filthy coward!'

She made a run for it.

In Passing

The man in the overall said: 'I've brought someone.'

She was sitting by the window. She looked up and saw him in the doorway standing next to Roelofs. He was young, he wore a check shirt with sleeves rolled up, his forehead was high, he had narrow eyes; grey, she thought.

'He wants to talk to Mark,' said Roelofs.

'Mark isn't there,' she said.

'Where is he?'

'At Gevers' stables, I think. He had to go there first.'

'I'll go and see.' Roelofs introduced the young man. 'He can wait here, can't he?'

She nodded and pulled her smock over her heavy belly. He went to sit opposite her, bending forwards, his arms on his knees.

'Would you like something to drink?' She pushed herself up with both hands.

'Don't go to any trouble.'

'No, I'll get it.' There's something about this man, he looks familiar. In the kitchen she leant against the table. She had forgotten to ask what he would have. She took a bottle of beer out of the fridge, picked up a glass and went back in. 'You don't come from round here?' she asked.

'No.' He drank some beer immediately.

'It's good cold, isn't it?'

He nodded. 'Lovely. I've been here a couple of weeks. Working.'

'At Roelofs' place?'

'Next door.'

She sat down again. Roelofs never says anything either, she thought.

'I've got a dog with me. I think he's ill.'

'Where do you live?'

'Amsterdam.'

'I thought so. I don't go there any more. When are you going back?'

'Tomorrow.'

'Already?'

He did not reply. He emptied his glass in long gulps. She saw his hands were a paler brown than his arms.

'Aren't you bothered by the heat?' he asked.

'No. I can take it.'

'Is the baby due soon?'

'In a fortnight.'

'Your first?'

'Yes. We've lived here for five years. I haven't been away since. Once you settle here you don't go away.'

He looked outside. 'It's beautiful here, that open country right by your door.'

'You don't see a soul here.'

'I never thought I'd find a vet in such a hamlet.'

'He's busy enough, he's the only vet in the whole area. That means whole days away, evenings too, and nights.'

'Are you always alone?'

'Often.'

'You've a splendid house.' He stood up and walked about the spacious rectangular room.

'It's old. Mark's grandfather built it. We've altered it a bit, of course. Do you want another beer?'

She rose and went to the kitchen. He went with her. She felt a pain low down in her back. Next it'll begin, she thought. But it passed.

'Let me get it,' he said when she opened the fridge.

'It's all right, it's no trouble.'

He had also reached for the handle, his hand brushed hers. He smiled. Round his eyes were lines that curved upwards. 'Are you drinking anything?' he asked.

'No, not now. What do you do?'

'I paint a bit.'

'How?'

He shrugged his shoulders. 'Come and see.'

'Where?'

'I haven't got anything special here.'

'You're really leaving tomorrow?'

'Yes, unfortunately.' He turned the tap on and off. 'I think you'd like it. I'm not thrifty with colours.'

She sat on the stool. She hadn't thought about the telephone any more. Mark said she must think about the telephone when he left in the mornings. In recent weeks she had done nothing else. All the time she went from the room to stand by the black object and imagined how she would phone, with the pain dragging through her body. She knew the line was often faulty. Sometimes the telephone itself failed to make any sound.

'If I had known, I could have come one day,' she said.

'Do you still go out of the house?'

'Why not? Shall we go and see the dyke? We can go along at the back.'

'Isn't it too hot for you?

'No. It's always refreshing there.'

She opened the kitchen door. They followed the narrow path that ran behind the house and rose to a dyke overgrown with grass and nettles. He took her hand and wanted to pull her up with him.

'There are some steps. I put them in there myself. Before, when I wasn't pregnant. They're completely overgrown.'

'Careful,' he said when they were at the top.

'I do this so often, it's not difficult any more.'

She went to sit on a bundle of reeds, her feet supported by a block of basalt. He stood looking towards the sea. Small boats with dark sails moved in the distance.

'They're the fishermen from the other side.' She held her hands round her belly. 'He kicked.'

'You shouldn't be alone so much when it's here.' He sat next to her.

'Is your dog very ill?'

'I don't know. He certainly gives that impression.'

'Then what will you do, if you're leaving tomorrow?'

'He can lie down in the back of the car.'

'What will you do when you get home?'

'Work a bit. And you?'

'Nothing.' Then: 'I think it'd be better if you go back now. I heard Mark coming home.'

'Won't you come too?'

'No, I'll stay here a little longer. Mark will go with you to look at your dog.'

He remained seated for a moment and looked at her, as he had in the room.

'Will you come back here?' she asked.

'I suspect I shall.'

She thought about it. 'You must come in the autumn.'

He stood up. His shadow fell over her.

'Can you find the way?' she asked.

'Once I've been somewhere I never forget it.'

He climbed over the dyke. She heard him jump down on the other side. She stretched out, pressed her ear to the ground and laid her hands on the underside of her belly. It was just as if she already carried him in her arms. There was a distant sound of car doors closing, an engine starting. He'll already be three months in the autumn, she thought.

The Major's Daughters

At half-past eleven the telephone rang. Mrs Elgerlee was busy at the back of the house. She had to go down a few steps and through a narrow passage to the room where the telephone was. She looked at the clock and lifted the receiver. It was her daughter Adèle.

'Why are you ringing?' she asked. 'Is something the matter?' Perhaps her new bicycle has been stolen, she thought, or perhaps she has fallen ill at the office. But her daughter's voice sounded excited, almost expressive. She even heard her snorting, so at first did not understand her properly. Adèle repeated what she had said. It was about someone coming for dinner. Mrs Elgerlee leant forward a little, as though now she did not want to miss a single word.

'A friend of yours, Adèle?'

'You'll see,' said her daughter. 'I thought I'd ring you early so you could bear it in mind for this evening.'

She did not ask her anything else and Adèle immediately brought the conversation to an end. The old woman stood where she was with the receiver in her hand. Now there would be a lot to do today. It was a long time since they had had a guest at table. It never happened any more. Her two daughters each led their own lives. Selien even more than Adèle. Selien was out the most and confided in her the least. It went without saying that they did what they wanted; they were old enough to do so.

Mrs Elgerlee sat down on the sofa. What had she been busy with at the back of the house? She could no longer remember, and nor did she want to get up and look. My daughters are old women, was her thought; but in her memory she saw two little girls in white dresses whom she sat with in the stand watching the parade. It was hot. The parade-ground seemed faded grey in the heat. The hussars' sweating horses stirred up clouds of dust. But they were seated high and cool in the shade of the projecting roof; they waved to acquaintances, leant forward as the troops approached. Look, there goes your father. At the head of the second battalion. Major Onno Elgerlee. No, he was still a captain then. Without his face altering its military bearing he greeted them with a gentle movement of his sabre. He walked with a hollow back, unbending. She had first met him at the cadets' annual ball. At the final ball he had danced with her all the time. She swayed gently back and forth now, arms stretched out, head back a little. Oh, she could have married whomever she wished; she always had men after her, pretty and cheerful as she was, she was invited to every party. She had often told her daughters about it. But they did not want to go to the ball. Go out with cadets? They turned their noses up at it. 'As long as I don't have to,' Selien always said. She had dragged Adèle along in her contempt for officers. Their own father included. Good, he had been strong, he had drilled his children, had regarded his house as an extension of the barracks. But that certainly would have changed if he had lived longer.

Her thoughts returned to the telephone conversation. Would Adèle finally. . . ? She had always seemed rather childlike. As when for example she went about with her new bicycle. It was a gleaming toy to her. 'I feel exactly like a girl of thirteen,' she had said. 'I imagine that everyone in the street is looking at me.' Perhaps her chances were not yet over. She had no illusions about Selien; she had so organized her life that there was no place for any man.

The old woman rested her head against the back of the sofa. Some flies flew round the lamp above the table. She recalled how she had come by that lamp. Before her marriage she had bought it in a little antique shop. It had originally been an oil-lamp; Onno had installed a gas mantle in it. Later, that was exchanged for a light bulb. Only the flies remained. Even if the lamp swung, whenever Selien stood up from the table in a fit of anger and bumped against it. She had had another violent outburst last week. And all about nothing. Adèle made a remark about her girl-friend. Selien criticized her for never having been in a state of friendship. She had no girl-friends, let alone a boy-friend. 'I've had plenty of boy-friends,' said Adèle. 'There were three who definitely wanted to marry me. Who would actually want to marry you?' It had been difficult to come between them that time. She is Onno exactly, thought Mrs Elgerlee, Selien is just like her father, short-tempered and stubborn.

'My son will go to the military academy,' Onno had said when she was pregnant for the first time. It always rankled with him that it was a girl, so much so that the arrival of the second child no longer interested him. The eldest ought to have been a boy in order to carry on the family tradition. He treated Selien like a boy. He spent far more time with her than with Adèle, but also punished her more often. What were they like as young girls, after all? she asked herself. She remembered that period less than their earliest years. It was as though she had missed out on a part of their youth or had grown old without altering. As a child Adèle had not had bulging eyes or that thick throat. Selien was different. She had Onno's pointed nose and tawny complexion.

She looked at the clock. I sit here, she thought, and I've still got to prepare everything.

Mrs Elgerlee was busy in the kitchen the whole afternoon. At last she could take the porcelain dinner service out of the cupboard once again. She dusted it off carefully. It was an age since it had been regularly used at table. Her husband often brought colleagues home for a drink and a meal. Then Selien and Adèle had to stay in the kitchen. She had once seen them try on the guests' shakos and march along the passage with stiff legs and a walking-stick and umbrella over their shoulders. They had never had respect for a uniform.

She had done everything by the time her daughters came home. Selien was early this time. Usually she appeared only after her mother and sister were already seated at the table.

'What's going on here?' asked Selien. She stood in the doorway with her hands in the pockets of her leather jacket, her short hair combed straight back. 'The table in full regalia?'

'We're having a guest,' said her mother. She was startled. She had heard Selien arriving, but because she had gone for a rest after she had laid the table, her thoughts had wandered again. 'A friend of Adèle.'

'Oh, come on,' said Selien, 'you don't still believe that?'

Mrs Elgerlee rose from the sofa and leant over a chair. With her finger she smoothed a wrinkle in the table-cloth. The silver and the crystal glasses shone. It was like it used to be. Voices and the jingling of sabres being taken off sounded in the hall. She had made the white wine sauce Onno loved.

Selien clicked shut her cigarette-lighter. As she walked round the table she tapped her cigarette with sharp little flicks and went to sit by the window to smoke.

'Shouldn't you change?' asked her mother.

'I can't think why.'

'Oh, I thought, so . . .'

'Couldn't we just as well have eaten off the ordinary service?' asked Selien. 'The man won't know any better. Perhaps he'll even be embarrassed.'

'Why do you think that? Do you know him, then?'

'Oh no. We never come face to face with these vague acquaintances of Adèle's. You've worn yourself out for nothing, believe me.'

'It's different this time,' said her mother. 'She really has invited someone now. A boy-friend, she said. Yes, that's what she said. He's coming to eat. Be pleased, Selien.'

'Why should I be pleased?

'That your sister's bringing a boy-friend home.'

'What are you carrying round in your head, Mother – a marriage, by any chance?'

The old woman stroked her hand over the chair cover. She was right. What have I got into my head? She will never marry. Can I hear her there? 'Here they are.' She pulled her dress straight and wanted to go into the passage.

'Don't get excited,' said Selien. 'She's alone.'

Mrs Elgerlee let herself sink into the chair. 'Everything's on asbestos mats.'

'Luckily,' said Selien.

'How was it at school?'

'Fine, ordinary.'

Did her daughter ever tell her anything about that school! She would have liked to hear what sort of pupils she had. Those children looked so nice nowadays. She always watched them when they passed in their short, coloured skirts, lively and open-hearted, as she herself had been as a young girl. She felt as though she were slowly drifting away. She certainly noticed that Adèle was in the room; she had even said hallo to her, but she forgot the laid table on which she was leaning her hand. The room grew vague. Her daughters sat opposite each other by the window. She did not recognize them. Who were they? They were old

women who reprimanded her because she had gone to the cadets'
annual ball, because she had been brought home too late again by that
young reserve officer in his black uniform. She looked at her hand on
the white cloth. You grow so accustomed to yourself; you don't notice
that your hands become old, the veins thick, the skin dull and wrinkled.
When would you be nearest to yourself? When you're young or like
now, old and weary? Why did she brood about it? What good did it do?

'How late will your friend be?' she asked.

'He'll be here soon.'

'From where?' said Selien. 'Where must they fetch him from?'

'What's it to you?' asked Adèle.

'You don't have to explain to me. I know those tricks.'

'He's coming,' said her sister. 'He's coming to eat. I've arranged it
with him.'

'Who is it, Adèle?' asked her mother. 'What's his name?'

'I'll introduce him to both of you soon.'

'The famous mystery,' said Selien.

'As though you don't have much more to hide with your girl-friends,'
said Adèle.

'I've already told you so often, you shouldn't meddle in that,' said
Selien. 'You don't understand. You think and feel like a child.'

'At least I've known men,' said Adèle. Round her finger she wound a
shawl she had brought in with her. 'How often I could have married . . .'

Selien laughed loudly. 'Do you hear that, Mother? Your daughter
Adèle could have had marriage after marriage. Why didn't you? You're
an old spinster now.'

'Just like you. And you're even older than me.'

'I don't spend my whole life waiting for a man.'

'Even last year,' said Adèle, 'you know, Mama, when I made friends
with that rich man?' She wound the shawl off her finger. She held her
head rather bent. Red blotches appeared on her neck. She felt them
coming up. 'He wanted to marry me. He was very nice.'

'Yes,' said Mrs Elgerlee, 'that's true. I remember your telling me
something about it.'

Adèle pulled the shawl round her neck. 'He wrote to me and tele-
phoned me, he fetched me from the office.'

'Couldn't we put a light on?' said Selien. 'I'd like to be able to read my paper.'

'Let's wait,' said her mother, 'until Adèle's friend comes. What does he do, Adèle? Is he an officer?'

'What makes you think that? You know quite well I've never looked at an officer.'

'Thank God,' said Selien. 'At least we're spared that.'

'But children, your own father . . .'

'That was already bad enough,' said Selien. 'I know how jealous I was of my school-friends because they had fathers with ordinary jobs who wore ordinary suits. I always found it a misery.'

'Selien! They have to be there for the defence of the country!'

'Stop it!'

'I don't understand it,' said her mother. She shook her head. 'Your father was such a good man.'

'He hit Selien with his sword belt when she put rice in his shako,' said Adèle.

Mrs Elgerlee sighed. 'Fathers beat their children. And, what's more, he would rather have had a son.'

Adèle sniggered behind her shawl.

'I do know it wasn't easy, but he could also be very nice to you. Didn't he often take you with him . . .'

'To parades, military exercises, barracks, rifle ranges, yes indeed. He brought us tin soldiers.' Selien rapped a knuckle along the length of the window-sill. 'He put them in battle order, he shouted commands and forgot his children. Shame that he didn't go to war. Then he could have put his games into practice.'

Oh dear, thought the old woman, they didn't fight here long, but he still would have shown what he was worth as a regimental commander. Shortly before his death he had proof again with his promotion to lieutenant-colonel. Who would have thought that such a healthy, strong man would succumb to pneumonia?

'Now, what's happened to your friend?' Selien folded the newspaper and beat it impatiently on her knee.

'We should at least see how late it is.' Mrs Elgerlee stood up and put the light on. 'Seven o'clock. That man really ought to telephone. It isn't polite.'

'Perhaps he can't find it,' said Adèle.

'You explained properly to him where we live?' asked her mother.

The table is pretty by the light of the lamp, she thought. I don't understand how they can't see that.

'Naturally once again it's just like those other arrangements with your so-called boy-friends.' Selien walked to the door with angry steps. 'Weeks ago you began going on about it to us. I have a friend, I'll bring him with me, he'll come and be introduced. And who have we seen here all that time? Not a soul. Fabrications, a carry-on, showing off by someone past forty behaving as though she's twenty.' She stood right in front of her sister. 'Give it up once and for all, Adèle. No man is ever going to come for you again. Put that idea out of your head for good and don't trouble us any more with your childish fantasies.'

'They aren't fantasies.'

'Don't lie!'

'Oh, how awful,' said Mrs Elgerlee, 'a napkin has fallen over. You mustn't bump against the table, Selien. I folded it so neatly. Before, if you went to the dinner at the cadets' ball and your napkin fell over, you had to kiss your neighbour on your left. There were girls who knocked them over deliberately.' Laughing, she looked at her daughters.

'What nonsense you always talk,' said Selien. 'Let's go and eat. I'm hungry.'

'She thinks I've never had a man,' said Adèle. 'She thinks I've never been to bed with a man. If only she knew.' Her hands made a waving movement beneath the shawl. 'Shall I tell you what it's like, Selien?'

Her sister walked to the door making a gesture of disgust.

'Stay awhile,' said the old woman. 'It's not that late yet.'

'I'll eat in the kitchen,' said Selien. 'I don't feel like waiting any longer.'

'Have you ever once felt like waiting for a man?' asked Adèle.

'Adèle,' said Selien slowly, 'I'll give you a piece of good advice.'

'No thank you, I'd rather not.'

The old woman was dozing off. Adèle heard her sister close the front door behind her. She went on sitting with the shawl in her hands. She had made a ball of it, pinched in as though it were a piece of dough. What am I doing, she thought, what am I doing? She looked at her mother. Her head had slumped on to her shoulder, her mouth hung half open. What will it be like when she's dead? Perhaps her life would then become quite different. Absurd of Selien to claim she was too old. Naturally she had invented that boy-friend, she was proud of herself, it had become a game, she did it as a way of conjuring: who knows, someone might actually come.

She walked to the kitchen and stood in front of the cooker, raised the lids of the saucepans, took a spoon and stirred the thick sauce that had congealed at the bottom. She put something from each pan on to a plate and ate standing up. It was still quite tasty, she found. She would never be able to cook like her mother. On Selien's plate a cigarette-stub lay in a circle of solidified fat. She put her plate on top of it and pushed it away. She saw a man shaving himself opposite through a window. She put the light out and continued watching until he had finished. Now the balancing act. In the dark she stood on one leg, closed her eyes, stretched her arms out sideways. Then she turned the light back on, found a cleaning rag and went to the hall to polish her bicycle. 'Ting' went the bell. It frightened her. She had rung it without realizing. She looked at her mother through a chink in the door. It seemed as though she had slid under the table. Only her head remained above it. If I stay here I'll be like that one day. And waiting. For whom? For what? She closed the door quickly.

'We must eat something,' said Mrs Elgerlee. She rubbed her eyes and blinked in the light. She saw that a napkin had fallen over again. Carefully she straightened it, smiled, rubbed her cheek and pushed the chair away from the table a little. Half-past eleven. She now remembered what she had been busy with that morning when Adèle rang. She had taken her husband's uniform out of the cupboard, brushed it and polished the buttons. She must put it away again. She would do so immediately. Before she went to bed.

The Friend

As the tram circles the station square I see him standing under the clock, directly in the sun, his jacket over his arm. His forehead is burnt red as though he has been waiting for hours. I stay sitting until everyone has got off. So, he has come too, like me he wants it to happen, today and other times; days Sander won't be at home; stolen hours.

Slowly I cross the square. I can still go back; he hasn't seen me yet. If I continue walking behind other people and inside the station I leave by another exit, nothing will have altered, Sander will have no reason to notice anything about me and I'll never have to hedge about anything when I'm home. But he suggested it himself. So why should I go back? This morning I got out of bed determined to go through with it. If Sander had had any suspicion of the chance he was giving us with this, he would never have started it. It didn't occur to him. One of the few things I'm now grateful to him for. It's true; I hesitated by the front door. I heard him singing under the shower. At that moment I thought: you may never see me back again.

I walk straight over to Frank now, faster, as though I want to make up for lost time.

'I've been looking out for you for a while,' he says. 'I thought you wouldn't come by now.'

'Really? Wasn't it agreed?'

'I didn't know whether you really wanted to.'

'Didn't you?'

I see he's looking at my red blouse. I was in red on that evening too and he thought it suited me very well. 'It's your colour,' he said. I wondered about that, because Sander had asked me again before we left the house whether I couldn't wear something more respectable.

Now I feel just how hot it is. There's a thick, sweaty heat over the asphalt. Blue exhaust fumes hang there. 'Shall we cross?' I look forward to the bustle inside the station, the hurrying for the platform, the tension while waiting in front of a ticket-office, one eye on the queue and one on the visibly advancing clock.

Frank guides me to the barrier. 'I've got the tickets,' he says.

I feel his hand on my arm. He lets go immediately. Angry elbows and hips push me through the gate. It doesn't diminish the childlike feeling of anticipation I always have when I travel. It's part of it. But when I see the crowd on the platform jostling for the train to the coast I ask myself whether we wouldn't have been better off going somewhere else. Actually I don't want to go to the sea at all. It's because of Sander. The three of us were at table. Frank had come to lunch. All I said was one day I'd like to go to the sea.

'Why don't you two go together?' Sander asked. 'You like it too don't you, Frank?'

'Yes, I like swimming in the sea.'

'Are you doing anything tomorrow?'

'No,' said Frank, 'not that I know of.'

'That's fine, then. I'm away the whole day tomorrow.'

Sander was buttering a slice of bread, careful to spread it evenly with the point of his knife. I was staring at a dish that had a piece missing. I break things a lot. Why is he forcing this all of a sudden? Does he suspect anything and does he want to see our reactions? I can't imagine he's saying it just to do me a favour.

'You heard,' said Frank. 'Sander's sending us on a day out.' He looked over to me and smiled.

We've known each other a long time. He's a friend of Sander. They studied law together. Apart from that one evening, nothing has ever happened between us.

'We'll have to stand,' he says.

'It doesn't matter.'

We are shoved on to the train with the crowd and now stand in a corner. A child presses the rim of his bucket into my leg. A boy who wants to pass by pushes me against Frank.

'You're not carrying anything. Are you really going to swim?'

'I've got my trunks on already,' he says.

A woman next to us looks at him as though he has disclosed a bedroom secret. How can we possibly find a quiet spot on the beach? I've never been alone with him before. Not even that evening about

three weeks ago. The three of us were at a party with friends. As it
turned out, Frank and I were rather at the back and no one took any
notice of us, not even Sander. He had done most of the talking as usual.
I'm used to his going on about one particular thing, wherever he is. I've
often reacted against it, and also to the way he usually takes the words
out of my mouth. Hastily, as though he's anxious someone else will
hear, he goes on with the word he's taken from me. I've had so much of
it that I don't say any more.

Frank and I danced together. 'I'd like to see you without Sander one
time.'

He had drunk a great deal and I knew it made him reckless. Me too.

'Does it make a difference?' I asked.

'I find it does.'

'Am I different, then?'

'Very different. Much more yourself, much. . . .'

He went silent. There was something wary in his eyes but his hand
went down my naked back, along the vertebrae. I pressed myself against
him; it was an experience for me to observe another man touching me
and allowing me to sense that my feelings were reciprocated. Sander has
always discouraged me from paying attention to other men. He domi-
nates me completely. I've never tried to withdraw from this lack of
freedom. I didn't know any better. It was easy.

But that evening it felt just as easy to behave as though Sander didn't
exist. That didn't alter later when he sat in front of us in the taxi. Frank
wasn't very concerned about him either. He gave me long kisses and in
the pauses for breath chatted with Sander, who didn't look round for
the whole ride.

After that he has kept coming over as usual, and although he doesn't
let what happened between us show, each meeting has a hidden tension. He never comes if I'm alone at home. Out of respect for Sander?
To wind me up? Or precisely because he doesn't want to compromise
me? I've no idea. But I've constantly had the feeling in recent weeks that
he, just like I am, is waiting for an opportunity, an unsought occasion.
Sander had to decide for us. Always Sander.

The train has already stopped a few times and it's become even more
cramped. We are now standing right up against one another. I feel his
leg pressing against mine and can't tell in this crush whether he is doing
it intentionally. Strange, it is as though I scarcely know him or don't yet

know anything about him. Perhaps after all it is a good thing we're going to the sea. The more people there are, the less you pay attention to each other. The strap of my bag pinches my hand. Someone behind me knocks against my head, untidying my hair.

'We're nearly there,' says Frank. 'I'll be glad to get some air.'

It sounds like a reproach. He stretches his neck, making him seem even taller. I turn my face away a little. Will he see me as 'different' again? There are beads of sweat over my top lip. And I must comb my hair.

We go through the narrow street to the promenade. Children drag their spades behind them over the cobbles. Girls with long brown legs saunter past. An ice-cream man disappears down to his shoulder in the container in his van. We stand by the railings on the promenade. The sea is smooth and grey-blue; the beach runs along it like an untidy border. We take our shoes off and go down the steps on to the hot sand. Frank is immediately some way ahead of me as though he is in a hurry to get to a prearranged place in the distance. I keep having to swerve aside for racing children, step over sandpits and over tent-ropes that my bag catches on, slowing me down.

Eventually, on the damp part of the beach, I can feel the sea breeze. I stop and call Frank but he goes on, apparently not hearing me. There is so much shouting. He said little in the train. Anyway it was too hot and too full. And I had great difficulty holding a conversation out in the corridor. Sander would have talked throughout such a journey. With him Frank only has to listen. He is more used to Sander. I try to catch up with him; I step in his footprints as often as possible and when he stops abruptly I knock into his heels with my toes.

'There are still a couple of tents free,' I say. 'Shall we hire one?'

'I can't see the attendant anywhere. But fine, let's go over there.'

When I unbutton my blouse he turns his back to me and fiddles with the belt of his trousers. He stands with his legs wide apart, broad-shouldered, head forwards a bit like someone on a sports pitch who sees a ball shooting towards him. I pull my swimsuit on under my skirt and roll it up. I hang my clothes on a peg, spread the towel out and sit on it. He lies next to me and shades his eyes with his arm. He has dark hair on his chest and his legs are thickly muscled. Now I must say something to him, but a man in a white sailor's cap saves me. He approaches us, making brusque gestures.

'This isn't your tent,' he says.

'No,' I say, 'but we'd like to hire it.'

'Impossible,' says the man sombrely, 'it is taken by a German family. They'll be coming.'

Frank sits up. 'Haven't you got another tent for hire, then?'

'Everything's taken,' says the man. 'All the tents are hired out for a month.'

We get up and collect our clothes. 'We didn't know,' I say.

The man looks at me as if I am telling the lie of the day.

'Shall we go somewhere else, then? It doesn't matter where,' says Frank.

'Won't it be quieter further on?' I look along the beach. There are people, sandpits, tents as far as I can see.

'If we walk for an hour perhaps. That doesn't seem much fun to me now you've got all your things to carry.'

He sticks his hands into his shoes and holds them out ostentatiously. I have to laugh but he doesn't join in. It was a serious complaint. It won't be so once we're lying down, I think. I drag the towel behind me. Next to another tent I throw everything down. 'Here, then.' I spread the towel out again.

'We've really picked a day,' he says.

'We?'

'Yes, true.' He laughs. 'Sander.'

'Otherwise you wouldn't have thought of going to the sea?'

'You're the only one who isn't keen.'

'I mean . . . with me.'

'With you?' He turns on to his front. 'I must honestly confess I'd never thought about it. Perhaps that sounds unkind, but it's Sander I'm always with. You know how long we've been friends – long before he married you.'

'Why have you never married?'

'I was married.' He says it gruffly and turns on his side. 'Sander would have told you that, surely?'

'I don't know anything about it.' Of course not; I hear such things only after everyone else is already in the know. But now I want to go on, I want to look behind that wide, tough forehead, behind that closed expression.

'Who were you married to and when?'

'Long ago, very briefly.'

'If you'd rather not talk about it . . .'

'Rather not. It was a rotten time.'

What difference can it make to me? Perhaps she walked out on him, perhaps he left her, or who knows if she died, from cancer or something like that. I lie stretched out and poke my hands deep into the sand. I burrow towards the cool.

'You two have a good marriage, anyway?' he asks suddenly.

'You think so?'

'Yes, surely?'

'Oh yes.'

I push my head into the towel, harder; it makes a dip, a miniature hiding-place. I hear the waves hammering, the sea is coursing under the beach, and my heart beating. Children cry. There is constant shouting. If only we were in the water.

'Shall we swim?' I ask.

He lies as though asleep. A woman in the tent next to us is undressing. She stands naked before she puts her swimsuit on. She is very white and fat. I touch his arm and he opens his eyes. His face is close to mine. I feel the heat is heavier, through my whole body.

'I'll wait a bit. You go ahead though.'

I go. He ought to come. He's annoyed because I wanted to ask him about his marriage. I walk carefully over the shells, over the hard sand-ridges, to where the ground becomes soft, past the bathers. Waves splash against my chest. I shiver, turn round and look at the beach. I can't see him anywhere. I squat down, push off and roll gently out until I can extend my legs and only my head is above the water. Sometimes the waves seem to be restraining themselves. I swim easily through smooth sea and feel the ripples on my body as though I'm constantly being caressed. The beach is far away now. I feel like shouting out loud, just to hear how my voice sounds here. But I don't know what. The only thing you can call from such a position in the sea is: help. And who'd help me? They can't even see me. Perhaps they think: there's a dead seagull floating, a piece of wood, a ball lost by a child. All of a sudden the sea becomes rougher, waves break over me, I take in a gulp of water. At that moment I hear the sound of a hooter. So someone has noticed me.

I swim back. It is difficult. I feel myself tiring. The man with the hooter is waiting for me. 'You were much too far out,' he says. 'The sea pulls.'

'Yes, I noticed.' I stand still, breathing hard.

'Will you remember that in future?'

I nod and walk on. In the water, I think, in the water I dare. I pick up a couple of shells and throw them back again. I see the current has taken me some distance past our place. A band arrives on the beach. Children throng round, girls dance, they hold on to each other's bare shoulders. There is no sign of Frank. He must have gone for a swim. I stayed away too long.

He is lying on the towel, with his hands under his head.

'You haven't been into the sea.'

'Not yet. I find it so crowded there.'

'Not if you go out far enough.'

'Why bother?'

'It's pleasant sometimes.'

'At that moment, perhaps. But if you've got to come all the way back?'

'You have to allow for that. You know it in advance.'

'It's dangerous to go out so far,' he says.

'I thought you wouldn't be worried about that.'

'You talk as if you knew me very well.'

'Is that so strange? How long have you been coming over to us?'

'What's that got to do with it?'

He's right: it doesn't mean a thing. I have stretched out and I can feel myself drying quickly. The sun beats down and penetrates. It's entirely up to me; with other men I don't know how to proceed, I'm not tactful, not refined. I met Sander too early to learn. I've turned into the person he wanted me to be.

A boy jumps over us. Before he dashes off he looks at me with a smirk. Frank dusts himself down.

'Are you covered in sand too?' At least I'm saying something.

'It's part of it. One of the day-tripper's pleasures.' He laughs. Finally he laughs again.

'It's easy for you to talk. But it's difficult to get it out from inside a swimming-costume. Next time I'll wear a bikini.'

He gets up. 'Just a minute, there's some in your eyebrows and round your eyes. Come here.'

He folds his handkerchief and wants to go over my face with it. I push the handkerchief away. 'That's full of sand too.'

He bends over me and brushes my eyebrows with his hand. I close my eyes and feel his fingers over my cheeks, my neck, my shoulders, under the straps of my costume. I listen, immobile, my body taut. The noise from the beach is very far away. He claps his hands together. I hear him lighting a cigarette.

'Did you arrange with Sander how late you'd be home?' he asks. He throws the match over his shoulder.

'No. You?' How long ago was it I stood listening to Sander's singing?

'Yes, more or less. We ought to go over a couple of cases. He said he'd have time for that this evening.'

'When did he say that?'

'Yesterday evening.'

'Was he at your place?'

'Yes, he dropped in.'

'What else did he say?'

'Do you want an exact account?'

'Was it about me?'

Of course he went back over it, over that evening. That's quite certain now. All that time he knew what I was longing for. He dealt with it again in his own good time. He could relax; he knows what his friend is like.

'No, I don't believe Sander mentioned you.'

So what? Most probably I'm mistaken. Other women manage to be all the time. They do so effortlessly, with a glance, an inflection. It is hot, too.

'Perhaps we could return now, otherwise we'll have to go in another packed train.'

'As you wish,' he says.

As you wish!

I go behind the tent to dress. My blouse is creased. Everything in my bag is covered in sand. My back hurts. I forgot to put cream on. My clothes chafe against my body. I prop my mirror up on a tent-ridge and comb my hair. Behind the canvas there is muffled laughter. Someone begins to play a harmonica. I pick up my shoes and go back round the tent.

Frank is also dressed. He stands waiting for me like he did this morning, with his jacket over his arm.

'Shall we go, then?' I say.

The Other Side

He had pushed his bed into a corner and laid cushions on the floor. The bottles and glasses were on his desk. Walking backwards to the door, he subjected the room to a final inspection. The painting with the sheep-pen! As he took it off the wall he noticed his hands shook. He put it at the bottom of the cupboard, on top of the old shoes, his father's tall black ones and his mother's dirt-brown lace-ups. His hair had fallen over his forehead; he combed it and went downstairs. In the kitchen he looked for dishes and a bottle-opener.

'How late are they coming, Karel?' his mother called out.

The living-room door stood ajar. He pushed it a little further open and looked round the corner. His parents sat at the table in a pool of light that reached no further than the backs of their chairs. The lamp-shade of painted parchment allowed the rest of the room no more than a soporific semi-darkness. His father was doing calculations with a pencil in a thick ledger. He was in his shirt, the sleeves held up by elastic armbands. It looked as if he had enormous biceps. His mother was shelling peanuts. She dropped the shells in a saucer and popped the nuts greedily into her mouth.

'Do you want to take anything upstairs with you?'

'No, I've got plenty up there now.'

'How late are they coming?' she asked again. She put her tongue between her teeth and upper lip and pushed the saucer of shells away. A brown flake stuck to the corner of her mouth.

'At half-past eight.'

'It's really nice for you that you've already got a set of new friends so quickly.' She nudged his father. 'Don't you think?'

His father looked up and nodded. He poked his pencil in his ear.

I must say it now, thought the boy.

'Yes,' said his father, 'you've settled in nicely over this last couple of weeks. You've ended up in a strange town at a new school. I'm not so

52

far on at the office. I've still only a few contacts.'

'We are very curious,' said his mother.

You always are, he thought. 'I've already been home with different people, but you know what it's like here with these parties?'

'You're being asked all over the place, eh?' said his father. 'You know how to make yourself popular. That's good. You need that in society. And you can have them here properly – you've got a nice room. Haven't I done it up nicely?'

'Very nicely.'

'You can count on your father.'

'Otherwise you could easily have brought them in here. You'd have had more room here,' said his mother. 'Your father and I would have gone and sat in a corner.'

'Oh no, that's too much of a bother for you.'

'Have you got enough to drink? And the savoury biscuits? Shall I bring them upstairs for you?' asked his mother.

'No, no, let me do it myself. The other people do it at home too. The parents never get involved. I've never seen them myself.'

'How unfriendly,' said his mother. 'Shouldn't you even shake hands with your children's friends?'

'If they prefer to sort that out for themselves now,' said his father. 'I can well imagine it. We'll say hallo in the hall, no more.'

'There's really no need,' said the boy. He went further into the room. He must finally get on with it. 'It's so crazy,' he said with a forced smile. 'They're rather . . . rather stand-offish, yes, perhaps you won't believe it, but it's a question of shyness. They're usually timid.'

'My goodness.' His father slapped his flat hand on his book. 'Timid! And they're grammar-school pupils. They'll soon be taking on leading positions. Lucky you've never had that problem. Your father and your mother have taken good care of that. You know what your grandfather always said: Upbringing, monsieur!'

'It's only an impression,' he said quickly. This was a mistake, absolutely wrong. 'Naturally it's because we're still new here, the town is bigger, people keep themselves much more to themselves, where we come from it was altogether more sociable, Mother herself said she has no idea what sort of neighbours we have, and you at the office. . . .' He spoke all in one breath, nervously searching for new explanations, credible arguments.

'Sure,' said his father. 'I'm not generally that quick at getting chummy with my colleagues, but if you approach people with a friendly manner you win them over. In our house no one need be timid.'

'I'll bring you a tasty snack,' said his mother.

'That always helps,' said his father.

'They won't be here that long.' The boy fidgeted with his jacket. 'As it's the first time they're coming here, stay in the living-room. That'll put them at their ease. They're quite used to that with their own people.' He had retreated half behind the door again.

'It's all right, we'll do as you wish.' His father bent over his ledger again. 'Timid,' he muttered, 'timid.' He shook his head.

'That's agreed, then,' said the boy. 'They should be here. I'll let them in.' He closed the living-room door behind him, collected the dishes from the kitchen and went upstairs. Luckily they didn't understand anything about it and in any case they now knew they mustn't make an appearance. Stupid of me to start on about shyness. What did I have to blather on about it for? Father fell for it. How is it possible? But Mother said nothing. If she comes up and produces her tasty snacks, for God's sake! He fetched the record-player and opened it. Now he chose the records.

'Look, Karel.'

He turned round with a jolt. He could not hide his bewilderment.

'No need to be frightened,' said his mother. 'It's me.'

'I didn't hear you. What is it?'

'I've just shelled a saucer of peanuts for you. They're always delicious.' Her eyes went round the room. 'Oh, where's that painting your father hung up for you?'

'I've put it in the cupboard for now. I was worried they'd hit their heads on it now I've moved the bed into the corner.'

Keep talking, there's nothing to it, I am scrupulous with nice things. Even now, when they immediately go back on it. He looked at his watch. 'Thanks for the peanuts, Ma.'

'Where did you get the cushions from?' asked his mother.

'From the attic. They much prefer to sit on the floor than on chairs. Specially the girls, it's informal, you don't have that sense of paying a visit. . . .' He made some airy gestures.

'Old cushions. You can't let them sit on them?'

'They're fine. Besides, I've shaken them out.' He held the door open for her.

'They've got dirty in the move. You can tell.' His mother bent down and turned one cushion over.

'Come on now, Ma. I think they're here.'

He heard voices in front of the house, the tinkling of bicycle bells, a girl's high laugh. 'Go downstairs now.' He gave his mother a little push.

'I'm going.' She raised her shoulders as though she wanted to shrug him off. Slowly she went out of the room. He had to restrain himself from hurrying her again. He walked down the stairs close behind her. The bell was pressed hard. He waited until his mother was in the living-room, closed the door and went to let them in.

At first he was on edge and listened all the time for someone coming up the stairs. But they kept to the agreement. His confidence returned. He played his role of host assiduously, provided everyone with drinks and cigarettes, put records on and danced with Yola, a tall blonde girl with grey, rather crooked eyes and a greedy mouth.

'Beautifully high on the legs, a thoroughbred,' Chris had said. He was partial to the expert's hearty clichés. He had been surprised he had to take so little trouble to get her. The first week he was at school he had already made a date with her and after an evening in the park he had to agree with his new friends. 'She's hot-blooded,' they had told him, 'a damned hot girl.' She had bitten him and he had come home with a swollen lip. Bathing it with cold water made no difference, his mother saw it immediately. It had cost him a whole story.

'This room's got something,' said Yola as they danced.

'Oh yes, it's OK.'

'You've made something of it. You can see the fundamentally bourgeois aspect of it coming through naturally.' She laughed and nodded in the direction of the windows. 'Those thick curtains. And that little table – appalling.'

He sighed and pulled a pitying face. 'I've been here too short a time to change everything radically. That'll come.'

'I could help you. Can you have me here alone, do you think?'

'They're not that bad.' He kissed her neck.

Chris and Leo smirked at him. They sat on the divan with Elsa between them. They tapped their cigarette-ash on to the floor. Lindt knelt by the record-player choosing records; her upper body swayed to and fro with the rhythm of the music. Her calves were too thick, he noticed. Peter sat at his desk reading a book. Now and then he looked up and flicked a peanut with finger and thumb in the direction of the group on the bed.

It's going well, thought the boy, I got myself into a state for nothing. He did once go to the stairs to listen, but everything down below remained quiet. They've gone to bed, of course. This lot better not make too much din when they go. Chris is capable of anything. At a pinch he'd walk in to the bedroom and then say: 'Sorry, I thought this was the toilet.'

When they broke up by half-past twelve he said: 'I'll go with you. I'll take Yola home. But please be quiet on the stairs, otherwise I'll catch it.'

'I'll take my shoes off,' said Yola. She leant on his arm.

'Give them to me,' he said. 'I'll carry them for you.' He looked at her narrow, brown feet. The toes with their red-painted nails were constantly moving. Everything about her body was eager, greedy; it made him anxious and at the same time provoked his infatuation. I wish we were outside, he thought.

They sneaked downstairs, laughing and calling 'Shh!' Chris scratched Elsa's back with his finger; she screamed. 'Quiet,' the boy called up the stairs. 'Keep quiet.' He stood in the hall with his arm round Yola, waiting for them. He switched the light on. There was no sound from the living-room. Now he knew for certain they had gone to bed.

'Here we are,' he said, relieved. Leo took his father's hat as he passed the coat-rack and pulled it low over his head, whereupon Chris commandeered his mother's, a black felt cloche hat with a feather. They took each other's arm and looked at the others with straight faces. 'Don't,' he wanted to say but didn't dare; he laughed with them.

He still had Yola's shoes in his hand when the living-room door opened and his parents appeared on the threshold. They had pale, sleepy faces. His mother's hair was dishevelled. He saw her sagging body; she always undid her girdle when it was late. His father had taken his collar off. In the mean light in the hall the stubble of his beard made him look shabby.

'Your father and I would like to make the acquaintance of your new friends all the same,' said his mother. 'Have you enjoyed yourselves? We heard you dancing!' She laughed and nodded at the group by the coat-rack. Just at that moment she discovered the boys with the hats, who could think of nothing better than to persist with their pose. The laugh on her face drained away. She was not sure if she should think this was funny.

'I thought your parents were in Athens,' said Peter.

'Wasn't your father an embassy secretary there?' said Elsa.

'Have you rented out rooms to your own parents?' Yola snatched her shoes out of his hand and quickly put them on. She was the first to go out of the door. Chris and Leo threw the hats on the rack and followed her. Peter was the last. He lingered, he looked inquisitively from his parents to him as though he wanted to assess the likeness. 'Until tomorrow,' said Peter. He closed the door loudly behind him.

'What do they mean?' asked his mother helplessly.

'Your son can explain that to you,' said his father. 'He's at the grammar school.' He moved his head forward a little and put his hand on his wife's shoulder; she leant against the door-frame, her arms folded beneath her low-slung bosom.

The boy walked past them. With head averted he went upstairs. He knew they were watching him; he hoped they would call him back and that his father would shout, strike. It could never be worse than the two words Peter had said to him: 'Until tomorrow'. Therein, sealed up, lay everything he was afraid of.

My Mother's Village

We drove into the village over a bumpy country road. It was an April afternoon, the sun shone but a strong wind blew, the frail leaves trembled on the trees and the grass on the verges slanted to one side as though a comb had been pulled through it. The driver muttered something and the last passengers got off. I buttoned my raincoat and turned my collar up. We stood on the village green, a little square with trees, surrounded by low houses. I walked past the weather-beaten pump whose grille was almost entirely hidden by a thick layer of moss and weeds. I grasped the handle and found it was completely rusted. The driver was eating a sandwich. When I got on at Delfzijl he had said, with a wink, I thought: 'So, all the way to the end?'

I had sat on the right at the front and saw he kept peeping at me in his mirror. It made me uneasy; I wondered whether he noticed anything about me, and tied the scarf tighter over my bleached hair. It could be unspoken understanding, ordinary curiosity or something quite different. But if he intended anything he would not be sitting quietly in his bus eating. I set out quickly across the green and turned into a street at random.

My mother had told me so often about the village where she had been born that I had thought I would recognize it. 'We'll go there one day and then you'll see how small it is,' she had said. But it never happened. It was too far, in the extreme north-east of Groningen. In the image I had constructed of the village there was a bandstand on the green with flower-beds and benches round it. And there, close by, my mother's house. A white house with green shutters. But the houses were grey and had no shutters. I walked through the village unnoticed. In the distance I saw women working in the fields. Their skirts billowed out in the wind. A boy sat on a doorstep writing with a piece of chalk.

'Where is the vicarage?' I asked. He looked at me without saying anything. I asked again. He put the chalk in his pocket and sauntered off down the road. I wouldn't call that friendly, I thought, as I followed behind him. At the corner he stood and waited; he signalled me to follow him. Here the street was badly paved and there were no paths up to the houses. The boy stopped in front of a house with a white painted gate, which he held open for me. It banged shut loudly behind me. Now I'd found it so quickly I'd be able to catch the return train easily.

The woman who opened the door said that the minister was not at home. I asked her if she expected him soon. 'I think my husband will be out all afternoon. He'll be back around supper-time. Can you come back then?'

'That will be difficult. I'm from Amsterdam and I must get back this evening.'

'Won't you wait?' she asked. She withdrew inside a little and held the door open wider. 'Couldn't you try? It's possible he'll be home earlier.'

It was my only chance. Perhaps I wouldn't ever be able to make the journey again, and if I could it would probably be too late to do anything about it. 'I would like to wait,' I said.

She showed me into a sombrely furnished room. 'My husband's study,' she said. Behind a large writing-desk I saw a bookcase full of black, leather-bound volumes. Those are the registers, I thought, they look like them. An old Friesian clock hung on the wall.

The minister's wife sat down in a low chair next to the fireplace and took up some knitting. She had a round, flushed face and dark blonde hair. She wore glasses with thin gold frames. At a particular angle the lenses reflected the light and her pale eyes became invisible. 'Do you know my husband?' she asked.

'No,' I said. My mother had once told me that as a child she often played with the minister's children. Their back gardens bordered each other. 'I've never been here before. You are rather isolated here.'

'When we go out of the back door we're right in the fields. It was certainly a change for us. We both come from the town. Five years ago my husband was appointed to this parish. I thought I'd never get used to it, but now the war's on we aren't that badly off. Better than where you are in Amsterdam, I imagine.'

'Yes, in Amsterdam life is difficult for many people.'

She nodded, put her knitting down and went out of the room. She wore flat shoes with rubber soles and straps over the instep. So, my mother's house wasn't at the back. I sat by the window. From the next street there was the sound of a farm cart, metal wheels over rough cobbles.

In the train a man had kept talking about his budgerigars. He had a ponderous voice; he spoke his words as though they were stuck to one another. He demonstrated with his short, pudgy fingers how he handled his budgerigars and touched them. It was just before Beilen that someone interrupted him. 'Westerbork is over there.' Everyone looked out of the window, including the budgerigar man. 'They become so attached to you, did you know that?' He addressed me. I had looked at him because I didn't want to look outside. 'No,' I said, 'I didn't know that.' Then he went on about the special features of his birds. I listened to his monotonous voice without hearing what he was saying.

There were a lot of *Grüne Polizei* on the platform at Assen. They walked alongside the train and looked into the compartments. 'Sometimes they get on and check everyone on the train,' said a woman. 'We're lucky.' 'We've nothing to hide,' said another. I clasped my bag. I hadn't yet needed the identity card. I hoped I wouldn't have to show it. Although it was a reasonably good forgery, it still didn't make me feel safe.

I noticed that even though I had arrived at my destination I continued to hold my bag clasped to me. I hung it on the arm of the chair. I was still so unused to a false name I was surprised the minister's wife hadn't noticed when I introduced myself.

She returned, just as noiselessly as she had gone out, with a tea-tray, which she put on a low table. She spoke jerkily, as though she kept having to search for the words or was thinking about something else.

'I hope it turns out better than expected, so your husband comes back earlier today.'

'Is it concerning something urgent?'

'Yes, very urgent.' I stretched my back. I felt as though I had been sitting huddled for a long time, with my chin in my hand, and my back was stiff. As a child I had to sleep on a board for a considerable time and wear a surgical brace on my shoulders. 'Walk-straight' became a kind of nickname for me. In Assen as the train left, commands had been shouted. The soldiers sprang to attention. There was a clattering noise. 'They fly right on to my fingers,' said the budgerigar man. 'I just have to tap on the cage and they come.' He imitated it on his knee. By that stage the best part of the journey was over. I thought it a good omen that there had been no extra delays.

'It's not for myself,' I said to the minister's wife. 'I want to speak to your husband about someone else. It is urgent.'

'I cannot reach him.' She had poured the tea and was knitting again, the needles tight under her arms as though she wanted to clamp herself to them. 'He's visiting various farmers, which always takes a long time. The farms here are far apart.'

The Friesian clock ticked sharply. I realized it was already too late to catch the train back. 'I'll have to wait now. I'd rather not give up.'

'You can stay the night here.'

I said I would like to, if she didn't mind. It was as though she blushed then. She had a tendency to turn her face away from me all the time. Did she feel ill at ease in my presence? But then why ask me to stay?

'If you had come yesterday you would have found my husband at home.'

'Yesterday?' I said. Yesterday I had just heard that the transports were being suspended for a week. Yesterday it had just dawned on me that there was still one chance to do something for them. I had lain the whole night thinking about how I would put it to the minister. It had to sound credible.

'You could have written too.'

'Then days would have been lost.'

She walked to the desk and put some papers on a pile. She stood with her back to me; the belt of her dress was twisted.

'Those must be the baptismal registers.' I pointed to the books on the shelf.

'No, they are kept in a separate bookcase, there.' It was a cupboard with carved doors and a brass key.

'I have come about somebody in the register.'

'Oh yes? For someone born here? Do you have family from here?'

'No, not that. It doesn't concern my family.'

'Just a moment!' She turned and raised her finger. 'I can hear something. I think he's definitely here.' Quickly she left the room.

I had been listening virtually without a break to all the sounds from outside; in the distance I had heard the constant tramp of clogs; children had called out, the wind had chased round the house. But this time I had not heard anything.

Someone closed a door. There were muffled voices in the passage. She would be telling him about me. I would have to pay attention to his face when he came in.

'It's about a couple,' I said, 'good friends of mine, who are in Wester-bork at the moment. The transports to Poland are being suspended for a week, I've heard.' I'd already repeated it so often to myself I could now listen to my own voice as though someone else were speaking. The minister sat behind his desk with his hands in front of him on the blotter. He had heavy, bushy eyebrows, a strange profusion in his narrow face. 'I believe there is still now a chance of getting them out of the camp. I know them very well. I must do something for them.' I looked at the wood-carving, a female figure with folded hands. 'They must get out.'

The minister picked up the figure and put it down again. 'You have come to see me about that?'

'The woman was born in this village. It appears that she's of Protestant descent. In any case, her maiden name isn't Jewish. You used to find it among the farmers in this district. She was brought up by Jewish foster-parents but it is very likely that she was baptized a Protestant.' I waited a bit. The figure was now in a different place. 'With a declaration that she is of Protestant descent and a certificate from the register, I can see a possibility of getting this woman and her husband released. They let mixed couples go.'

'It is no trouble to look.' He picked up a pen. 'Tell me what she is called and when she was born.'

I said my mother's name and the date of her birth. He wrote it down, went to the other cupboard and took down a large book and began to leaf through it. I saw that the pages had yellowed and were curled at the edges. They were written in a thin, sloping hand. 'It can be quickly checked.' He went down the pages with his finger. 'Everything is arranged precisely by year.'

I followed his finger. Suddenly I had the feeling that it was true. He would find my mother's name any moment now. Look, there she is, there's her name. Carefully written in the year 1890.

'Strange,' said the minister. 'I can't find it. Could you be mistaken? Are you sure about her date of birth?'

'Yes, I'm certain.'

Now he went to look in the other registers. 'Don't lose heart, she could well have been baptized later.'

Although I was prepared for it and knew what I had to ask him immediately, I delayed it because I wanted the strange tension in me to continue. But not for too long. He walked with the books to the cupboard, put them back and turned the key.

'That name doesn't appear in the registers.'

I noticed I had been sitting hunched for too long again. 'Could you give me a declaration all the same, then?'

He stood with his hand on the cupboard door, half turned away from me. His wife counted the stitches on the full needle. The Friesian clock was almost at the half-hour again. It doesn't matter, I thought. I must say to him that it doesn't matter whether her name is in the book or not. Papers are what count. They'll easily get out of the camp, take a train, walk in the street, go inside their own house. From the way he suddenly looked at me, turning his head to me with a little jerk, I could tell he saw through the deception I was guilty of.

'There's a real chance that with it I can save them from deportation.'

'I would like to help,' he said. 'If it was up to me I would indeed give you that declaration. But I cannot decide alone. I must discuss it with my church wardens. They must be in agreement and sign it too.'

The waiting began once more. The minister got back on his bicycle to convene his church wardens. First we ate something in the kitchen at the back of the house. The minister's wife spotted that during the meal I kept looking outside. She nodded to me and said she too liked that open view. I had the impression she was much more lively than in her husband's room, as though she could now be more herself.

'Do people often get out of Westerbork in this way?' she asked, when we were seated again in the study.

'Oh yes. As long as you have official papers with signatures and stamps. That's what the Germans are rather sensitive about.'

'You hear such horrible things nowadays. It's getting worse all the time. They think they can find something even in this backwater.'

'Do they make house searches?'

'Yes, sometimes. But they never come to the vicarage.' She was quiet, gazing ahead, and then she looked at me with her blue eyes, in front of which the spectacle lenses now shone gently. She smiled. 'You are doing a lot for your friends.'

'I have a lot to thank them for.'

'Couldn't anything be done for them before they were taken?'

'It happened so suddenly. There was a raid in their district. The streets were roped off. All the Jews were dragged out of their houses. There was no escape.'

'Do you still live with your parents?'

'I live in lodgings.' I heard a shutter banging somewhere. The wind was still blowing.

'I lived in lodgings once too. They are often so cold, aren't they?' Her gaze moved round the room. She looked at her husband's papers, at the fire that she had made up for the evening and which now burned low, at the tray of cups from which we had drunk tea, coffee and tea again. 'They ought to do it.' Her voice was soft. Rather as though she said it to herself.

But they did not do it.

They held their hands behind their backs and their caps in their hands. I sat behind them. There was a smell of earth in the room, of manure and cattle. They had left their clogs behind on the doorstep and stood in their black socks in front of the desk. They turned their caps round and round, their dark-lined fingers moving inside the brims, to the peak and back again.

'Does this name appear in the book?' asked one of the church wardens.

'No,' said the minister, 'the name is not there.'

'Weren't they Protestants, then?' asked the second warden.

'There is nothing to prove it.'

'Then how can we make such a declaration?'

'It's not right,' said the first.

'I have already said to you that we ought to do it in order to help someone,' said the minister.

'What is not true is not true,' said the second warden.

'It's yes or no,' said the minister.

'No,' said the first. 'In that case we cannot sign.' All three shook their heads. The third had not said anything. He walked close behind the others as they left. They shuffled right past me in their socks, out of the room. The earthy smell lingered. It was as though the room was full of it, as though the clock now had difficulty ticking in the heavy air. As though everything now sounded more subdued. The gate clicked shut behind them. They had been inside only a few minutes. I had scarcely seen their faces.

The minister's wife sat motionless in her chair, her hands in her lap. The minister leant against his desk. 'I regret,' he said, 'that I cannot now do anything more for you and your friends.'

A few days later I received news from my father via someone I knew. 'We've been taken out of W,' he wrote on a postcard that he had apparently thrown from the train. 'We're on our way to the border. Mother is doing well. The train is very full.' He had written in pencil and hadn't signed underneath. It wasn't necessary. I recognized his handwriting anyway. No signature could add anything to it.

Only the Books

The moment the hard banging on the door got through to her she thought: There they are. But a few moments later she opened her eyes and knew the war was long since over. She looked at her watch. It was still early, not yet eight o'clock. She lay there and worked out for herself who or what it could be. Perhaps it was Dirk. But he could get in; he still had a key. She got up and pulled on her dressing-gown. The banging persisted, it became more violent. Dirk didn't come early in the morning. He didn't come any more.

'Were you fast asleep?' said the man. He wore a light-brown overall and had a coil of rope over his shoulder. The rubbish-bin was on the landing. She had forgotten to carry it downstairs the evening before. A plank and pulley had been propped against it at an angle.

'What have you come to do?' she asked. She clutched her dressing-gown tightly at the top and leant over the banister to look down at the doormat to see whether the post had brought anything. There was nothing there. The street door was open. The man had gone into the room and put the rope on the floor; then he came back to fetch the plank. She walked inside after him. He didn't hear her, he was busy unwinding the rope. She was almost sure she had already experienced this once before: a strange man silently brought certain objects to her that had an ominous significance. But she could not remember when it had been. She had never seen the man before and the things he had with him said nothing to her. Meanwhile he had gone to the window and opened it. Cold air flowed inside. She pulled the dressing-gown tighter round her.

'What have you come to do?' she asked again, now a little louder.

The man hung the pulley on the hoisting-hook, pulled the rope over and turned to her. 'To pack books. We've come to pack up a couple of cases of books.' He leant over the window-sill and called down something. He had a red face and bald head with a little frizzy grey hair on either side above his ears.

'Books?'

'Don't you know about it?' He took a note out of his pocket and showed it to her. 'That's here, isn't it?'

'Yes, I see. I didn't know they would be removed.'

'Here, I've got the address they're to be taken to.' The man wanted to show her another note.

'Never mind. It's all right.'

'Didn't they warn you?'

'No.'

She took a chair and went to sit in a corner of the room as far as possible from the window. The removal man hauled packing-cases up and put them in the middle of the room. He had fixed the other end of the rope to the plank with a loose knot. She wondered whether Dirk would still come to say which books had to go and which could stay. Some of them were hers. She could still pick them out. They were mixed up, her books among his. 'Otherwise it becomes such a chaotic mess,' Dirk had said. 'There must be a definite order in your bookcase – not one work by a writer here and another there.' The man had already taken a pile from one shelf. She let him get on with it. Carefully he made small stacks in the packing-case, which he had first lined with a cloth. He pushed the spines gently, like a book-lover passing along his bookcase.

'You do it very carefully.'

'It's necessary with books. Then they can be put in the bookcase in the other house in exactly the same order. Take it from me. The people don't have to bother about it.' He went to the shelves to fetch a new pile. 'At least, if they keep the same order in that different house. But why shouldn't they want the same order in a different house? That wouldn't be logical, don't you think?'

She nodded. 'They should go exactly like that in the bookcase, I think.'

'I wasn't told I had to take the bookcases too. Are there some there as well?'

'Perhaps.' She had no idea what it looked like there. He must have enough space, otherwise he wouldn't be having his books moved.

'A nice collection,' said the removal man. 'We get to know in our work.' He closed the packing-case with a clamp, which he fixed with a little piece of wood.

'We were just beginning.'

He didn't hear her through the noise from the street; the angrily hooting cars in a jam, a motor bike kick-started with palpable determination. She had fewer books than Dirk, but between them they had a lot. During the war they had sold everything of value for food, cigarettes and books. They had even got rid of the typewriter and their watches. They lived near a church tower and could see the time out of the rear window. 'When the war is over we'll buy everything new,' said Dirk. She saw him rolling cigarettes – he called it 'constructing' – from stubs that had already been stubs. They read, the oil heater between them, their books as close by as possible. In the end they no longer went out of their house. Now she often thought – and then she felt a flush over her whole body so that the cold sweat crawled on her back – she thought: I wish the war was still on.

'There we are.' The man had lowered the packing-case out of the window. 'Doesn't anything else have to go in?'

'No, only the books.'

'I only ask. We always pack the chests half full with books and then put light things on top, clothes and suchlike. It's a shame not to use the empty space.'

'I wouldn't know what else should go.'

She saw the thick whirls of dust on the empty shelves. She had never cleared the books from them. 'Dust preserves books,' claimed Dirk.

'People never move just their books,' said the man.

'No?'

He had taken something with him every time. She behaved as though she did not notice it. Also he usually came precisely when she wasn't in; as though he had waited in the street for his chance to sneak upstairs unobserved. It was after the period when they had continually discussed whether or not he should leave her. Generally it ended in a trivial row. The removal man began on his third case. She wanted most to go back to bed, to pretend to sleep. Like that time he came home in the middle of the night. She had lain listening to footsteps in the quiet street. They had always passed by. He did not put any lights on, he tiptoed; he fetched his suitcase out of the cupboard and packed his clothes in it, carefully, without rushing. He said nothing, as though he knew she lay awake. She had to get used to sleeping alone. Later, when he did not come any more, she slept better, she stayed in bed longer than she ever had, often letting the morning go by and sometimes the beginning of the afternoon too.

'It's almost done,' said the man. 'You see, packing goes quickly.'

'Not unpacking?'

'That depends. If the stuff isn't in a mess in the new house, it's sorted out quickly.'

'It isn't a new house.'

'Well, in that case. . . .' He stood with the lid of the last chest in his hand and looked at her. She stubbed out her cigarette in the ashtray, felt the glowing butt on her finger-tip. He shrugged his shoulders and closed the lid with a bang. 'So it's only the books. Nothing else at all?'

'No, nothing else.'

She stood up after he had lowered the packing-case. He unhooked the pulley, threw the rope down and put the plank over his shoulder. 'I'm leaving you with all the mess.'

'That isn't the worst.'

When he had gone she leant out of the window. The rope had left wide smudges on the window-sill. It gave her a feeling of relief to see the man stow the plank and rope inside the van and close the door. She still did not know why all this was so familiar to her from before.

The van drove slowly down the street. It was a yellow van with black lettering. On the other side of the road a couple of children walked arm in arm carrying satchels. A man pushing a cart stopped and spat in his hands. The clock tower struck. The children began to run.

She turned round. She was aware of how grey the room was, with the unmade bed, the mouldy walls and dust everywhere on the stained floor. She tried not to look at the bookshelves. I can hang something over them, she thought, I can put something else in them, I can get rid of them, yes, I'll get rid of them. She got a broom and swept it over the empty shelves, swept the floor, went on sweeping until all the dust left in the room was together in a grey heap.

She closed the window and went back to bed. She would have to stay there a long time to get warm again.

Return

He could not get to sleep. He lay awake for hours. It was hot. He drew the blankets carefully aside and made sure Rosa did not notice. She slept with her arm on top of the cover. A pale-pink arm. He had warned her again not to stay in the sun too long. She always laughed about it. 'I haven't got such a delicate skin as you.' During their time in hiding they had almost never seen the sun. They lived in the attic of a farmhouse, which had only one small window, high in the wall, made opaque with whitewash. In the evenings it was meticulously blacked out. Once or twice each day he stood on a chair to look out. With his nail he had scratched a peephole the size of a cent in the whitewash. Outside, a little of the country road was all that was visible, a wide bend lined with poplars.

'A woman's going by,' he told Rosa. 'She's about thirty. A boy on a bicycle. His ears stick out. A hay-cart. They're going to do the milking. Two children with a box of vegetables.'

It had become an established game. It passed the time. Sometimes he stood motionless at his look-out post, holding his breath. A grey, amphibious German troop-carrier sputtered along the road. A truck full of soldiers appeared, a whole column. The walls vibrated. Once, two soldiers came to the farm for water. He didn't budge. He didn't say a word. Rosa, who sat with a book on her lap, stared at him. She held the page she had intended to turn between her fingers. The incident lasted five minutes but days later they still saw it in each other's eyes.

A fly kept buzzing above the bed, just over his head. He didn't dare swat it for fear of waking Rosa. Now it was on the screen. He saw the dark speck creep on the gauze and fly off when a beam of light entered from below. It must be from the shed in the neighbours's garden. He heard footsteps, a door creaked, something was being pushed. The man was often busy in the shed. Definitely a handyman, someone with a hobby. He didn't know what he did. They lived right next door to

70

them. Rosa had minded when the previous people went away. She had liked the young children who had played in their garden, whom she would fetch inside if the weather was bad. When the new people arrived, the first thing she said was: 'They haven't got any children.'

The removal van came from The Hague. That must be where they were from. People from large towns didn't get involved with their neighbours. They weren't used to it. Rosa stirred. The large patch of light in the room bothered him. But if he drew the curtain across the window it would be too muggy.

The day they were able to go outside again for the first time it had been oppressively hot in their hiding-place. The window didn't open. They heard the farmer's wife calling loudly, running along the passage, up the stairs. Suddenly she stood in the middle of the room. 'Come out,' she cried. 'Come out, come outside!'

Rosa dropped a cup on the floor. She clapped her hands in front of her face. 'It's not true,' she said.

'What's not true? What is it?' he asked. He felt cold. He shivered.

'The Germans are surrendering. I've just heard. It's really true. Come outside quickly with me now!'

Of course they knew about the Allied advance. They knew it could happen any day. But now that it had actually gone that far he was afraid of it. What ought he to do? He wanted to go outside, and yet he didn't want to.

They walked in the road taking short, stiff steps. The war was over; you could see by the flags hanging from windows, by people wearing orange and red-white-and-blue. A boy went past playing a trumpet dreadfully out of tune. His face was purple. A cart full of whooping children came up behind them. Arm in arm, trembling in the warm sun, eyes blinking, they wandered along the road towards the village.

'We are walking here now,' he said, 'outside, normally. We can come and go as we please.' He listened to his own voice. It was as though he hadn't spoken aloud in years.

'Where are we going to?' said Rosa.

'Just for a bit of a stroll.'

'Let's go and look at the village. Have we ever been here before?'

'Not as far as I know.'

'It must be lovely round here.'

'Yes, it looks it.'

They had been there for two and a half years without seeing anything of it. They had arrived on a winter evening after a long train journey. They hadn't felt at ease in the compartment, with their false identity papers and their silent escort. They were the only ones to get off at the little station. He hadn't been able to make out the name of the place. It was another half-hour's walk to the farm, along dark country roads. They had held hands.

'It's just as if we're on holiday,' said Rosa. She had grown thinner. Her skin was sallow. There were wide grey streaks in her dark hair. Her shoulders sloped forwards. He'd never noticed that. They passed by a stationery shop. Rosa stopped. In the window on a base of faded cardboard was a pyramid of twisted paper decorated with little orange flags and surrounded by photographs of the royal family. But she was looking at the picture postcards that hung in front of the window, one beneath the other. Brown cards from long before the war, in which everything looked improbably peaceful.

'Look how nice it is here.' She reached up to look at the card on the top.

'Buy some.'

'Shall I buy a folder of them? How many are there in a folder?'

'About twelve, I think.'

'To send, you mean.'

He did not answer.

'To whom . . . who should we send them to?'

'They're for you. To keep.'

While she was inside the shop he waited by the window. He saw himself in the glass. An old man in an ill-fitting jacket. It had become much too large for him. A man with thin hair, with bags under the eyes; weary, from doing nothing, from waiting. He stretched and took a deep breath. His head now came a little further out of the roomy collar. He put his shoulders back, pulled his arms down at an angle and planted his feet firmly on the ground, until he felt tension and creaking in his body.

Rosa came out of the shop. 'Are you doing gymnastics?'

'Just a little, yes. I certainly need to. It's been a long time.'

'Two and a half years.'

'It seems three times longer.'

She put the cards in her bag. 'All the same, it's over now?' Her hand went to his sleeve.

'Come, let's go and sit on a terrace somewhere, in the sun.'

'If they've got anything to drink.'

'They probably have here. Ersatz coffee or lemonade, it doesn't matter what. It's the idea.'

'Yes, we're allowed to again, aren't we?'

They walked on slowly, looking for a terrace. He had the feeling that there was something he had known about for a long time, which he was now certain of, but that had not yet sunk in with Rosa. Or was she just pretending? Didn't she want to admit what she too suspected? That it wasn't really over. That for them it was just beginning.

The fly stayed still somewhere. Perhaps it was on the side of the bed. Below, the light remained on. There was a scraping noise, as though something was being rasped. That was how he felt. The time that followed had been harder to deal with than the years in hiding. Days when they scarcely dared to speak to one another, when they avoided using certain words. Many words now had a double meaning for them. The neighbour dropped something on the stone floor. Presumably he had a work-bench in the shed. Who knows, maybe his wife doesn't like him tinkering during the day so he does it late at night when she is in bed.

They remained in the village for a few more weeks. Transport could not be found back to their own home immediately. They were given another room at the farm and the people did all they could for them. He was in more of a hurry to be on his way than Rosa. He went into the village every day to find out whether he could telephone long distance or could send a telegram. The man behind the counter said the same thing every time: 'You must be patient, sir. They're working hard to get everything going again.' He folded his hands under his head and stretched. Rosa moved restlessly in her sleep. Ought he really to get out of bed and draw the curtain?

When they returned to their own town, three families appeared to be occupying their house. They had to stay with acquaintances. It was not easy to get hold of a house. People went to a lot of trouble for them. They could choose between temporary accommodation until something became available or find a home in a place nearby. They chose the latter. It was a small house. At first Rosa asked him what they would do about the sleeping space when the children were there again. He did not know what to say to that. She had eyed him for some moments.

'But look,' she said, 'one day all of a sudden they'll stand here in front of us. Jacques was never as strong as Stella but he's got a good head. And we need have no doubts about Stella, she was trained through and through.'

He dared not look up as she said it. He knew she herself did not believe it. She said it for him, and to adopt a kind of manner for herself in order to remove some of the tension between them, or just for once to speak their names normally, as they used to. He always used to watch when Stella was playing in a competition. It was during the summer before mobilization that she had beaten a well-known English tennis player. 'That girl's tremendous,' said the man next to him in the stand. 'She's my daughter.' 'Then I congratulate you.' That same summer Jacques had taken his final high-school exams and was going on to study economics at Rotterdam.

They did not come back. Nor did the other members of the family. The letters from the Red Cross were definite. Still, they had gone to look at the lists you could inspect at the office. He went down the columns with his finger. He did it only as an acknowledgement; to discover familiar names, because they were already on the list of those who would not return. There was nothing left of the sizeable Jewish community where they lived. The few young people who had survived had emigrated illegally to Palestine. Yet the mounting emptiness exerted an attraction he could not resist. He regularly returned to the town by bus. He told Rosa he had to put his business in order. He had to think about his business again. Vriens, who had looked after things during the Occupation, had already been to see him a couple of times. And when he heard that everything was as it should be, he felt more or less superfluous. Formerly he would never have thought of leaving things to others; he wanted to be involved in it all; nothing happened without his knowledge. So now he hesitated as he stepped down from the bus. Ought he to go to the office? He had done so once. Mostly he wandered in other directions. He searched. For points of recognition, houses, streets, shops. One day he went to look at the former synagogue. They'd turned it into a warehouse. The house next door, where the rabbi had lived, was now a business.

Sabbath mornings brought to mind the men with their high hats, the handshakes in front of the entrance, subdued talk in the vestibule. He stood in his place with the talles round his shoulders and his hands supported by the ledge in front. He smelt the leathery sweet smell and looked up, to Rosa and the other women behind the rail. A delivery van came to a halt in front of the high pavement. A man in an overall walked to the main door, which was opened only on special occasions, if there was a wedding or the chief rabbi came to visit. The door swung back and, creaking on its hinges, knocked against the wall. Another man appeared, carrying a pile of boxes from the van. He looked past him into the inside. Packing-tables were set up in the empty space. The back wall, where the holy ark had been, was taken up with racks. He walked to the side-entrance. Crates were stacked against the wall that bordered the rabbi's garden. Sometimes, if he had to be in the meeting-room behind the synagogue, he heard the rabbi's children playing in the garden. Stella was often there. When she went on the swing he would see her face appear up over the wall. She called to him and he would wait until she came up high again, the head with flying hair far forward, and then they waved to each other.

He stepped into the hall and asked one of the men: 'What sort of business is this, in fact?'

'A paper goods wholesaler. Van Resema.'

'Has it been here long?'

'Long? Oh no, a couple of years. There used to be a synagogue here.'

'Oh yes.'

'Are you looking for anyone?'

He said no and walked on, along the street under the large towers, where the wind always blew, past Samson's textile factory, now a bicycle shop, and the chemist Meier's, which was being carried on by someone else. He went in and asked for a tube of peppermints. A thin woman in a white overall served him. He took out his wallet slowly. He wanted to ask the woman something. She put her hand out; all of a sudden he had difficulty distinguishing between the coins – as though there was something in his eye – and gave her a guilder. As she handed him his change, she turned away to face someone who had come up beside her behind the counter.

Reluctantly he left the shop. He wandered across the square where the butter and egg market had once been. The butter hall was now used by the local music society for practice, so he had heard. They had been able to retrieve most of their instruments from German hands and wanted to put on a performance as quickly as possible. Why not? Now and again he encountered people he knew. At first he stopped to talk with them for a while. But as there was little variety in the conversation he now tried to walk past.

'Ah, Mr Goldstein, you here again?'

He said yes.

'How are you?'

He said he was well.

'And your wife and children?'

He said that his wife was also well. The children. He shook his head. There was silence for a moment. Then they asked about other members of the family from the town. Again he shook his head.

'Do you still live on the Singel?'

He explained that he no longer lived in the town, but in D, where they were content. And then they gave him their best wishes for Rosa.

At the corner was the post office where he sometimes took his mail on Sunday mornings. And the Singel was across the bridge. He had avoided it after their first visits to their old neighbours, but now he struck out over the bridge and walked by the water, looking at the house he had lived in for more than twenty years. Lace curtains in front of the windows, pot plants, a window-box. Woodwork painted brown. It used to be white, he thought, but he wasn't sure. It all seemed unfamiliar to him. He moved his gaze to the water, where a duck swam along followed by five ducklings. With his hand resting on a tree he looked at his house again. He studied it from the doorstep up to the roof and he had the feeling he was someone else, not the man who had lived there. Who was it who had seen his children being born behind those windows, had seen them grow up, hummed along with their jazz records, had danced at parties with his daughter's girl-friends? Was he that man? He oughtn't to stay so long, it would attract attention.

At the end of the Singel he crossed the road and returned along the pavement. He passed his friend Alex's house and could not understand it: he remembered everything about this one. The green, leaded glass of the top window, the plate with the house number whose '8' was so worn it looked like a '3'. The brass bell-push. The grooves in the stone doorstep. At the door of his own house he could see three name-plates.

Two next to the bell. The top one said *W. Witgans*. A card had been fixed underneath: '3 rings'. The second occupant was called Doorman; the third had placed his name-plate above the letter-box: *L. Spijking*. He didn't know them.

On the day he had closed the door behind him for the last time, he had said to Rosa: We'll be back within a year, perhaps sooner. Rosa had left the house as she had at other times, whenever they went away for a week. First she checked everything: if the gas was off, whether she'd switched off the mains, if the passage window was on the latch. In the kitchen she stood in front of the cupboard with a packet of biscuits in her hand, until he called her to come and to leave the packet behind in the drum. They walked along the Singel to the station with their escort without looking round.

A few times he had also visited the café he used to go to regularly with Alex in the market square. Nothing had changed. Only the smell of beer was sharper, he thought. The waiter who brought him his coffee behaved as though he had been away for a month. Questions about his wife and children, where they had been in hiding, how the business was. It was all the same. But he continued to roam through the town as though he were searching for something, as though he expected one day to meet someone who had something entirely different to say to him, the point of which he would understand. He passed the house where one of Rosa's sisters had lived. The end house in an avenue, next to a meadow. She had been a librarian and unmarried. A witty woman he had liked to talk to. The front garden was neglected; planks and piles of bricks lay there; grass and weeds sprouted up in between.

On Saturday mornings he walked home with Alex. They discussed the service, the text that the cantor had taken, how he had sung that morning. They had been at the same school and went on living in the same town. They had given each other advice about business matters and had helped each other when financial difficulties arose. He would have been able to talk about it with Alex, about the things that remained unsaid between him and Rosa, the subject they deliberately avoided. But perhaps it could be described in a few words; perhaps a passage that alluded to it could be found in the Talmud, which would point to an answer to the why that would not let go of him, which would never release him.

One morning he went into the town park, to the little restaurant near the pond. When the children were still small, they had often gone there. Stella and Jacques always made for the playground straight away. The weather was chilly, the light was grey. They played in the sand-pit. A mother with a woollen scarf on her head sat on the stone surround smoking a cigarette. The children did not seem to mind the cold. They hastily shovelled their buckets full, baked sand-cakes or built castles, just as his children had, just as he himself once had, watched by his mother.

'Mr Goldstein! How are you? I haven't seen you for ages.'

A tall man with a goatee beard came towards him. He did not recognize him, but didn't let it show. He indicated the chair opposite him and ordered coffee. While they talked it suddenly came to him that it was Mr Visser, the music teacher, who had given Jacques and Stella piano lessons.

'I thought about you just last week. Isn't that a coincidence?'

'That is a coincidence, yes.'

'I heard that you don't actually live on the Singel any more.'

'No. We live in D nowadays.'

'Not an unpleasant place, very quiet.'

That was what they tended to say: 'Not an unpleasant place.' He detected a certain chauvinism in it. It made him resentful.

'Do you recall you came round to us once when I gave a concert at home with my pupils? Your son was very gifted. He was my best pupil.'

He nodded. He said he remembered it.

'We still live in the same house.' Mr Visser drummed with his thin fingers on the table. 'When I returned, it rather surprised me that my wife was still there.'

'How do you mean? Were you taken away?'

'Yes. Didn't you know? One year in Vught, one year in Buchenwald.' He laughed. Red patches appeared on his thin cheeks. 'That's how it is.' He stirred his coffee. His pointed beard, going very grey, touched the edge of his cup. That emaciated face, and that beard. It explained why he hadn't immediately recognized him. They drank their coffee, they were silent. He felt the connection between this silence and the one at home.

After a little while he said: 'Are you giving lessons again?'

'Certainly. I run a music school here. I always wanted to do that.'

'How was it there?'

Mr Visser looked past him. 'I think back over it as little as possible –
at least I try to. It's not so easy.' He stood up. 'I'd better be going.'

He watched the thin man who moved away from him with slightly
jerky steps, as though he were mechanically defective. The sun came out
and shone on the table. When he went outside, a child with two hands
full of sand stood in front of the entrance.

'Would you like a cake too?'

He was meant to take it. 'Thank you,' he said.

With the moist sand in the palm of his hand he walked past the pond,
across the path with the benches. He saw a woman on the humped
bridge. It was too late to go another way. He prepared himself for all
the questions. She came towards him.

'I thought you were at the office.'

'Rosa, what are you doing here?'

'I could ask you the same.'

He let the sand fall though his fingers, rubbed his hand on his jacket
and took her arm.

'Have you been here before?'

'A few times. But never for long. I always had to make sure I returned
on an earlier bus than you.'

'Have you been all over?'

She nodded. 'And I've even met people who knew me.'

'What did you talk about with them?'

'I don't talk much with them. Of course they ask about everything.
They'd really like to know all the details.'

'I know. Would you like to live here again?'

They crossed the bridge. He pushed her gently up, then held her back
as they went down. She wore a black winter coat with a large collar.
Black used to make her look young.

'No. We're all right there, don't you think? And we can return now
and again, if we want to.'

'Do you sometimes feel the need to see everything here again?'

'Sometimes. Then I walk across the Singel, through the streets in the
centre of town. I look at houses and stand in front of shops.'

'And imagine how it was before?'

'I try to see it as it is now.'

'Why? To compare?'

'Because we returned. Because everything goes on as usual.'

She was further on than him, or did it only seem so? Strange that they hadn't bumped into each other sooner. He wanted to say something about the dismantled synagogue, about her sister's house and about Mr Visser, that he had been in various camps, but he said: 'You're right. Shall we take the bus back together?'

'Yes, let's.'

They went out of the park to the bus-stop. When anyone greeted them and wanted to stop, they just greeted them back and walked on.

He looked at his watch. It was nearly one-thirty. What did the neighbour do all that time in the shed? They really ought not to hold themselves so aloof from everyone, especially not from their neighbours. The wife seemed quite nice. Why didn't he have a chat with her one day? Words pass easily over a garden wall. There is always a way in: the weather, the plants, the new grass roller he'd ordered, the condition of the tomatoes, of which there were so many, too many for them. It would be a shame to have to throw them away. Eating and drinking. You can get everything again. Nature goes her way, things come out of the ground, disappear into it and sprout up again.

Now it was quiet down below, though the light was still on. Could he have gone to bed and forgotten to switch it off? He turned his head and listened out for whether the man was still there. And then he heard it. He sat up with his hands on the bed-cover. 'Rosa,' he whispered. 'Rosa, can you hear that?'

He heard it clearly now. The neighbour was whistling. He whistled something that used to pursue you virtually every day. He knew a couple of lines: 'Die Fahne hoch, die Reihen fest geschlossen, SA marschiert. . . .' How could you remember such words? The whistling sounded faint, almost hissed, as though it wasn't meant to be overheard. Why did this man whistle the Horst Wessel song in the middle of the night? He felt very hot, there was sweat on his forehead, his neck, his back. Did he whistle it because it just came to him by chance? But who exactly was it doing this now? The war had already been over for eight years and he guessed he was in his mid-thirties. An ex-Nazi who hadn't been free for long? Eight years. Then he must have done something serious, perhaps he had been in a senior position, had betrayed someone. It was possible. But when people are alone, often they do the strangest things. When they think no one can see or hear them they pull faces in front of the mirror, stick their tongues out, conduct an invisible orchestra, use words they would not otherwise dare say out loud, whistle songs no one wants to hear again, but whose melody lingers. Most probably this man doesn't even know what he's whistling. Why immediately think the worst?

He looked at his wife. He was glad she had not woken. He lay down with the blankets over him. He wasn't hot any more. He should try to get to sleep. He would think further about it in the morning. He had upset himself about nothing. In the morning he'd get to the bottom of it and then it would turn out that his first idea had been mistaken. But what difference did it make whether he was right or wrong? Nothing was altered by it.

Finally the light in the garden went out. But the whistling continued.

The Day My Sister Got Married

On the day my sister got married I rose early, even before my alarm clock, which was set for seven o'clock. I went to the window, half on the latch, pushed it further open and leant out.

A woman in a pink dressing-gown came to her kitchen door in bare feet. Cautiously, as though trying out the first ice, she took a few steps on the flagstones towards the garden path, whereupon she went back in quickly, raising her legs high. It was still chilly but the greyish white light was already beginning to break and it looked as though it would turn out to be a sunny spring day. Two gardens further on someone let a bucket tumble over a path. A red tom-cat balanced on the edge of the fence. Perhaps it had given that intense shriek in the middle of the night, which had startled me into waking. First I thought the sound came from the house. I lay quiet, listening, but heard no more. Everyone seemed to be sleeping peacefully. For a moment I thought I was in my room in our old house. That often happened to me these days. Anxiously I had to look at the door and the window, which here were in a different position seen from my bed, to realize that it had been a dream. I heard it again as I closed my eyes and turned on my other side. It came from outside. It was the penetrating squeal of a tom-cat and I did not understand that I had taken this sound to be a human scream. I shivered from the morning cold that came inside and closed the window.

'May is a lovely month to get married in,' the grocer had said yesterday as he put a large box of provisions on the kitchen table. And the florist had also remarked that he made the most brides' bouquets in this month. 'Weddings still take place. That goes on as usual.' It was early May 1942 and we had been wearing the stars for a few days. We weren't intending to have a proper wedding celebration, but my mother thought we couldn't let it pass us completely and should invite a few members of the family. 'Who knows,' she said, 'how long it will be before we all have another chance to be together?' Many of the family could not come, several aunts and uncles. It wasn't like it used to be at our larger house in Breda, where every opportunity was seized to ask as many people as possible.

If it had been left to my sister, all they would have done would have been to go to the synagogue for the marriage service, nothing more. I believe she thought it would be a godsend to get married in Amsterdam at the registry office without any of us there. A week before the wedding-day she rang up to ask me if I would take care of her bride's bouquet. 'That would be much easier for us,' she said. 'Then we won't have to bring it with us from here.' I promised to go to the florist the same day. 'What kind should it be?' I asked. 'You choose something you find suitable,' she said, as though it was self-evident that I had experience of that sort of thing.

I went downstairs and found my mother already busy in the kitchen. 'You're early too,' she said. 'That's good, there's still masses to do.'

'It won't be that big a do.' I looked inside the box of hired glasses. 'How many people do you reckon actually?'

'Oh, you never know. We could always have more than we thought. And perhaps they'll bring friends with them from Amsterdam.'

'She didn't say anything about it.'

'They don't have to. She knows everyone's welcome here.'

'I wouldn't know who might come with them.'

'Oh well, we'll see.' My mother gave me a tea-cloth. 'Just wipe the glasses.'

She went out of the kitchen. I had a strong feeling that she wanted to go on as though nothing had changed, as though she would have a house full of guests. She would walk through the rooms again and imagine how it always used to be: furniture moved to the side, long rows of chairs, tables pushed against each other, vases of flowers everywhere. And my father seemed to go along with this notion because I heard him say: 'I'll unlock the outside door, then they can push it open with their knees.' It was a standard joke of his.

The bridal bouquet was ordered early. It came in a rectangular box with a ribbon round it. I took the box upstairs to my room and put it on my bed without opening it. What had possessed me to choose those particular Japanese blossoms? Things always bother me. I'm rather superstitious. I seldom walk under a ladder, I pay special attention to things that happen on the thirteenth, even more so if that day also happens to fall on a Friday; I add up numbers I'm dealing with to see if the total can be divided by eleven or thirteen. I check myself in the performance of simple tasks in the house to convince myself that I have done them properly, not out of a sense of duty, but because I think that otherwise something dreadful will happen to me. I leave the bathroom and go back again to make sure I have turned the tap off, even though I'm almost sure I've done it. I half open a window, go to bed and get out again to see if I have put it firmly on the latch. But I had had no foreboding about choosing the bouquet. Before I went inside the florist's I hesitated in front of the window. I still had no idea what I should get and as soon as I was inside and saw all the pots of spring flowers I hadn't the faintest idea what I ought to pick. The florist, a ruddy-cheeked man in a light brown overall, inquired whether the bride was wearing white.

'She's not going to be in white,' I said.

I wasn't yet wearing the star. The regulations would come into force a few days later. So he couldn't know that we had any reason to keep the wedding celebrations modest. As he put some green stems in between a bunch of freesias he asked what the bride would be wearing and, because I didn't answer immediately, he turned to me in such a way that it seemed he made a small bow.

'Is she wearing a long gown?'

'I don't think so.'

'Then do you know what colour her gown is?' he insisted, 'as then I can take into account how the bouquet will match.'

I shrugged my shoulders. I couldn't enlighten him about that either. I hadn't asked her. It was a long time since we always dressed the same, as only a year separated us. My mother had certainly tried to keep it going as long as possible. She let out the same pullovers and skirts for us, we wore the same coats, even our shoes were identical. Only when we left junior school did we no longer have to go about as though we were twins.

The florist advised me to have small orchids. He frequently made bouquets with them and they were also chosen as buttonholes for the wedding guests.

'I don't think buttonholes will be worn.'

The heavy scent of flowers in the shop made me anxious. I felt that if I went on hesitating he would force on me something I really didn't want. He had brought a large vase of orchids out to the front, bent down and held a couple out next to each other for me to see the effect.

'Very nice.'

At the back in the shop I discovered on a platform a stone pot with branches of small, star-shaped, pink blossoms. I asked him what they were.

'That's Japanese blossom.'

'Can you make a bouquet out of it?'

'I can put together bouquets from everything here. That's not the point,' he said. He looked thoughtful. My choice probably struck him as unusual and I quite understood that he would rather have used orchids. But I thought those Japanese blossoms suited my sister exactly. He admitted that such a bouquet had never been requested. The bride certainly had highly individual taste. He promised me it would be quite special.

Although I was rather curious about it, I waited to open the box until my sister had arrived. I wanted to take her upstairs with me as soon as she and Hans got there. But my mother prevented us. We had to go in first, where an uncle was waiting with a present for her. It was my Uncle Herman from Assen, an exuberant little man who had taken the first train in order to be with us in good time. He had a black hatbox with him, from which he took his top hat. He held it with the inside towards him, made a couple of swift hand movements and began to pull something slowly out of it. It was a piece of blue silk which, just as in a conjuring trick, seemed to have no end. He let it flutter in the air and then draped it over two chairs as he watched us triumphantly.

'We can make at least two dresses out of it,' said my mother. She stroked the material, exactly down the centre where there was a crease.

'Or an evening dress with a train,' I said.

'I don't think she needs an evening dress now.' My mother folded the material up carefully.

'Perhaps for after the war,' said Hans.

'Of course,' said my uncle, 'it is pure silk. You can always keep it. The Germans won't hold out as long as all that. Mark my words.'

He took a flat brush out of his bag, smoothed the hat with it, put it on and went to sit opposite my mother at the table. To show how many bales of wool and silk he still had in the warehouse of his textile business, he made imaginary piles with his hands and looked up. Even if the war lasted for two more years he would be able to keep going with his stock.

I extracted my sister from the living-room. She had kissed my uncle on the cheek but had not said a word. Upstairs I pointed at the box on the bed.

'Your bouquet's in there.'

'What's it like?'

'I haven't looked yet.'

'Why not?'

She took her coat off and put it on the bed.

'I wanted to wait for you.'

She undid the ribbon and took the lid off the box. A sweet scent came out. Carefully she unwrapped the tissue paper. The florist had tied the bouquet with pink ribbons and worked in foliage of various colours. My sister took it to the mirror straight away.

'What do you think? Should I hold it like this?'

'I think so.'

'What are these flowers called?'

'Japanese blossom. I didn't know what you were going to wear.'

'That's as it usually is. It matches quite beautifully. Wait, I'll do it properly.'

She took out of her bag the little veil which is required for the synagogue service, put it on and went back to the mirror with the bouquet.

'How do you like it?'

She was wearing a light-green, long-sleeved dress cut straight, making her look even slimmer than usual. Her auburn hair curled out from beneath the veil. She had always been much smarter than I, and that often made me jealous. I envied her because she had far more boy-friends from school who came for her, who waited everywhere for her, who elbowed each other aside to dance with her at school parties.

The doorbell rang. I heard loud voices in the hall, doors closing, my father greeting someone, and through all that the whistling of the kettle. I sat on the bed and moved aside her coat, on which the star was visible. I turned it over. 'You look good,' I said.

She walked back and forth a few times in front of the mirror, almost striding, like we used to do in the attic with an old curtain on our heads and a feather duster in our hands as a bouquet. I wondered if she too now remembered how as teenagers we had imagined such a wedding. We took our creations from the films that we saw: Lilian Harvey and Willy Fritsch who waltzed their marriage in under enormous chandeliers, and Ginger Rogers and Fred Astaire who promised to be faithful to each other for ever as they tap-danced on a mirror floor. It was not long ago; it seemed so only because the war had happened meanwhile.

My sister laid the bouquet on a chest, removed her veil and folded it up.

'What are you doing now?'

'You don't think I should go on wearing it?'

'Oh no.'

'I'm not going to wear it outside. I'll put it on there, just by the door.'

'Yes, I understand.'

'How long a walk is it?'

'About ten minutes. A carriage maybe wouldn't take as long.'

'A carriage?'

'I mean. . . .'

She looked at me surprised, the veil folded small in her hand.

'Do you think in normal circumstances we'd get married with that sort of hoo-ha? Not for us.' She laughed and put the veil next to her coat on the bed.

Someone came upstairs. It was Hans. He wore a black suit and held a prayer-book I had seen him arrive with, still clutched under his arm.

'Do you always have that with you?' I asked.

'I'm afraid I'll forget it otherwise.'

'It looks like a beautiful one to me.'

'It was my father's. He gave it to me.'

It was gilt-edged, bound in heavy leather. On the first page above the Hebrew title there was a name in Gothic letters and beneath it *Berlin 1910*. Hans came from Berlin, where he had studied law. He couldn't complete his studies and in 1933 he fled to our country with his mother. His father, a well-known heart specialist, had given his private clinic to the city of Berlin at the end of the twenties. He died shortly before the handover. Hans was a Zionist and a factory apprentice and farm worker because he wanted to be qualified to go to Palestine.

After my sister became engaged to him she gave up painting and went to work in Amsterdam as a nurse. She had left everything in her attic studio, her painting chest, paints and brushes, canvas stretchers, panels, an easel spattered with coloured crusts of paint. On a trestle-table portfolios full of drawings, her canvases turned round against the wall. 'I'll come and fetch this gear later,' she had said. 'Perhaps in Palestine I'll get the time to do it again a bit.'

At home we weren't all Zionists. I once went with my sister to a meeting in the little room over the Breda synagogue, where girls in blue-and-white dresses danced the hora and sang cheerful songs. We weren't too inclined to get involved with the movement but later, under Hans's influence, my sister became more committed.

'How do you like the bouquet, Hans?'

'Lovely flowers. Just like little stars.'

'Only these are pink.'

'There's something else in the box,' said my sister. 'A buttonhole.'

'He did it all the same. I told him it wouldn't be necessary.'

'Who'll have it?' She held up the stem wrapped in silver paper.

'Give it to me,' said Hans. 'That's what it's meant for.' He fixed the buttonhole to his lapel with a safety-pin. 'Come downstairs. They're asking for you.'

'Don't forget your book.'

They went downstairs, chuckling.

While everyone stood in the hall putting on their coats, another aunt and uncle arrived from Zeist. It was rather a crush because my uncle blocked the others from the door. He had to tell them something. The fact that his wife, Aunt Mien, was not Jewish, had muddled him when he had completed the census form for the population register. Inadvertently he had written that he had two Jewish grandparents. 'But I went to correct it a few days later,' he said, then chortled as he pointed to the star on his chest.

'You could have tried,' said another uncle.

'I'd rather not have any unnecessary troubles round my neck.'

'I said that too,' said Aunt Mien. 'It's better like that.' She had a glum, rather crooked mouth, which twisted even more when she brushed invisible bits of fluff from her star-free coat.

One by one they went outside. I wanted to be the last and closed the door behind me, but I remembered something and went inside again. In the hall I stood for a moment under the almost empty coatstand. I opened the living-room door. There was a smell of cigar-smoke and coffee.

The length of blue silk lay neatly folded on the sideboard, next to Uncle Herman's hatbox. I went to the table, where there was a full ashtray. A cigar-butt was still smouldering. Half a cigarette had been stubbed out and bent over. Slowly I walked to the door, leant my back against the frame and looked round me. The silence in the room gave me a feeling of constriction, as though I were in a house to which no one would return. The irregular line of chairs gave the impression of being hastily pushed back.

In the hall I picked up my gloves, which I had left lying on the table, and hurried out. The others were almost at the end of the road. At the front my father and uncles walked with their black top hats, as they did every Saturday going to the synagogue. Then my mother and the aunts in their dark coats, my brother, taller than the others, a black stetson rather askew on his head, and his wife on his arm in a light beige suit, her jet-black hair in a bun at her neck. The bride and bridegroom strolled slowly after them. A few people stopped on the opposite side. One man took his hat off, a couple of children turned round, a curtain was held aside. As I walked faster to catch them up, I had the same sensation as I had in a frequently recurring dream: I am racing after someone in just such a sunny road and I can't reach them because the distance keeps lengthening even though the other person doesn't increase his speed.

'They do it in Amsterdam too,' said my sister when I had come up beside her. 'Yesterday there were even people who shook hands with me in the street.'

'How awful. I think I would have held my bag in front of it.'

'You mustn't do that,' said Hans. 'That way you can get into big trouble.'

We were now repeatedly being greeted by passers-by and I saw that my mother nodded back in a friendly way as though she knew all these people. In front of the synagogue door in the narrow street there were a couple of acquaintances waiting for us who went in with us. We didn't have to go upstairs, to the women's gallery. The marriage service is the only time the women can stay downstairs.

The synagogue wasn't half full, and that gave the ceremony a private quality. We stood closely gathered round the canopy, under which the bridal couple sat on special chairs. It was as though we wanted the circle we formed around them to screen them from the outside world. I thought of the game we played as children. In Holland there is a house. The lord who chooses a wife, my sister of course. They stand together in the circle and we drone on with the lines about the child and the maid and the servant and all the things that are chosen, until finally the house catches fire or is pulled down.

My sister's face was hidden beneath the veil so I couldn't make out her reactions. Neither did I ask her how she felt. She continued to look very beautiful for the rest of the day but also somewhat remote. And after that I had no opportunity to talk to her about it. Three weeks later, in the first raid in Amsterdam-Zuid, she was dragged out of the house with Hans and put on a transport.

My mother was very moved throughout the service. She had to use her handkerchief all the time. I knew her so well in that respect. She was always quickly upset, not only by family matters. The sight of the Queen also provoked strong emotion in her. I remember when I was a child that Wilhelmina once drove through Breda on a visit. We went to friends who lived on the route to watch the procession passing by. As soon as the party came into view with the Queen and the Queen Mother Emma, tears streamed down my mother's face.

She had frequent cause on that wedding-day too. As soon as we came out of the synagogue and my brother took photographs: of the married couple in the open door, where my sister still had to keep her veil on; of the couple with the parents, and one shot of the whole family. I had the impression that the large white handkerchief was never away from her face, but when I saw the prints later she seemed to be smiling all over.

'Now you,' said my Uncle Herman to me.

'That will cost you another length of silk.'

'Gladly. I've still got a whole bale of white silk, of the most beautiful quality.'

'I'll give you plenty of warning. I always wanted to get married in white.'

'She's still waiting,' said my mother.

We were at the table. I was next to my Uncle Maurits from Delft, my mother's brother, a long, lean man with a lorgnette. He taught French, German and English and also knew various dialects of these languages. Apart from Cockney and a Berlin patois, his favourite thing was potatoes. We called him the 'potato-eater', and when he came to stay with us my mother always gave him the best kinds, each of which he could name after a few bites. He stayed as thin as a rake and we imagined that he did not get enough to eat at home. Aunt Hilda, his wife, German by birth, was not only extremely thrifty but kept her husband strictly under her thumb. She looked very German, broad hips, flared skirts, her plaited hair firmly rolled over her ears like headphones. Their two children, a boy and a girl with their father's intelligence, were soon in the picture about the political events in Germany and could discuss it like adults even though they were very young. The household had little *joie de vivre*. Whenever they went on a trip to Scheveningen, my aunt and the children went by tram and, in order to save one fare, my uncle had to follow on his bicycle. He told us he could easily keep up with the tram because there were many long stops. It enabled him to catch up and his children, who stood on the platform of the second coach, could then often wave to him. He had cycled a good deal in his life. In the school holidays he sometimes came to Breda with two panniers full of books. He sat reading the whole day, his long legs on a chair on which he had first put a newspaper, while my mother was busy peeling potatoes in the kitchen. He corresponded with us on postcards, which always had the same opening line: 'We sincerely hope everything is to your satisfaction.' Even his last card, which he had written a few days before he and his family were taken, and which reached me alone, because the others had meanwhile been deported, began with this sentence.

My father tapped on his glass and stood up. At his very first words I saw my mother reach for her handkerchief. My father was an accomplished after-dinner speaker and he had no difficulty giving a picture of my sister as a child. He compared her distinctive qualities and character traits with those of Hans, and by means of many Hebrew texts fitting for a wedding, came to the conclusion that it was an ideal match. He closed with a toast to their future in Palestine. After we had all emptied our glasses there was silence. He had said nothing about the circumstances of the war. I looked round the table, where we sat rather cramped in the small room, the chairs pushed close to each other so that we constantly knocked into each other's elbows as we ate. After the war I could see that full room in front of me. For a long time I had trouble going into a room full of people.

The silence was broken by Uncle Maurits with a speech full of French and English expressions, which he translated to make it easier. He predicted that no one would be able to say of the newly-weds 'married in haste, repent at leisure', an expression the family really took to.

After the meal the bride and groom went back to Amsterdam. My sister picked up her bouquet, which had been on the table in front of her. One aunt advised her never to throw it away. 'You must dry it,' she said.

'I'll take good care of it,' my sister promised.

'You normally put it in the linen cupboard.'

'No, you must hang it over your bed.'

'I wouldn't like to be in Amsterdam now,' said another aunt.

'You're better off in the provinces.'

'It doesn't make much differerence where you are.'

'You shouldn't say that. There are far more Germans walking about in the city.'

'They're everywhere,' said my father.

'Let the children go to Amsterdam in peace,' called my Uncle Herman. 'What's going on now?'

My sister and Hans had gone and everyone else was standing round in the other room drinking coffee. I stayed at the table. I didn't think anyone else had seen. In any case I didn't let it show how shocked I was when my sister picked up the bouquet. It's a bad sign, I thought, as I looked at the pink flowers remaining on the table. A bride's bouquet should not shed its flowers.

My aunts came to clear the table. It became increasingly bare, the last glasses went in to the kitchen, the last dish, the napkins, the knife-rests, until on the white table-cloth, which was scattered with crumbs, wine spots and bits of food, only the pink, star-shaped blossoms remained. They seemed to have faded already. I went on looking at them, sniffed them and noticed that they also no longer had any scent.

'Lift your arm,' I heard. Someone folded the table-cloth together and carried it away like a sack to shake it out over the rubbish-bin. As I stood up I saw some of the flowers on the floor next to her chair. I stepped over them and went to my room. The box was still on my bed with the lid on. I took it off and held the box to my face. The scent was still there.

The Mexican Dog

Mr Kuisters at the fishmonger's, where some Friday afternoons I had to fetch salmon for my mother, was a lanky, bony man whose face consisted mainly of wrinkles. His head, with its stiff ginger hair, hung forward between his hunched shoulders. He cut the salmon with a narrow knife worn away in the middle, took the pieces between thumb and forefinger and laid them cautiously on one another. His hands were purplish red and scales stuck to them. Each time he asked me whether I would play with Tonia. And I said I couldn't because they were waiting for the salmon at home.

But one day I couldn't get out of it. The shop was busy. As soon as Mr Kuisters saw me come in, he pushed open the sliding door between the shop and the living-room and told me to go through because it would be a while. 'Tonia is home.' He shoved me between the shoulders and closed the door behind me. The room was small and dark. Tonia sat at the table looking at her hands on the plush table-cloth in front of her, a pale child with light, watery eyes and flaxen hair. She sat next to me in class and because everyone thought that she not only looked like a fish but stank of fish, no one would play with her.

'What have you come for?' she asked. She put her hands in her lap and looked at me suspiciously. Her mouth hung half open, her white face gleamed as though it were smeared with grease.

'I've got to wait here for your father.'

The furniture in the room was so crammed together you could scarcely move without touching something. I pushed the chair I was leaning on with my forearms as far into the table as it would go, but whenever I moved backwards I could feel the key of the sideboard sticking in my back. The space was made even smaller by an enormous fringed lamp that hung like a parasol over our heads. On the mantelpiece was a black metal clock topped with a little naked man. He held a kind of club in one hand and pointed down to the clock-face with the other. The mechanism ticked loudly. And we didn't say a word to each other.

After about twenty minutes Tonia's father came in. 'Here we are,' he said. He locked the door on a hook and changed his white coat for a brown jacket on a hanger in the cupboard. 'Now we can get on in peace.' He pushed two chairs aside, the only way to get to a low table in the corner of the room. On it was a radio set with a black ebony front panel. Coils stuck out and beneath the two knobs was a calibrated dial. Mr Kuisters pulled down a lever at the side, put the coils into a particular position and asked his daughter if there was a new fuse in the switch-box. She nodded.

'Lovely,' he said, 'then we can begin.' He looked at his watch. 'It's just the right time. Come here.' He beckoned to me, pulled a chair closer to the table and signalled to me to sit on it. 'Head forward a bit.' He stood behind me and gave me a light push on the top of my head; his hands went through my hair. A tremble crawled over my back, I felt it down to my bottom. I smelt a sharp fish odour, which made me feel sick. The man put a double metal band on my head and pulled two black discs with holes over my ears. 'Now listen carefully,' he shouted, 'it's coming now.'

He bent forwards so that his large, collapsed face hung right in front of mine. I saw the red blood vessels in his wet eyes and how his pupils darted here and there – he wanted to see what I was hearing. A tremendous noise started up in my ears, crackling, squeaking, a tearing yelling, long whines that suddenly changed into furious shrieking, which went through my whole body. Mr Kuisters laughed. 'That's him now,' he yelled. 'That's the Mexican dog.'

I tried to take the discs off but he held them tight, pushing hard on my head with his hands, and he turned one of the knobs.

'This is the Hilversum Wireless Station,' said someone and, after a few incomprehensible sentences, deafening music blasted against my eardrums as though my head was crushed into the horn of my father's gramophone.

After a while Mr Kuisters released me roughly from the head-set. The effect appeared not to please him. I sat there numb.

'Move over.' Tonia pulled at my arm. 'I'll have a go now.'

I stood up with ringing ears and throbbing temples and went to the door. I undid the hook with difficulty. Fumbling, I pushed the door back along its runner. In the shop the fish smell was stronger than ever. I dared to breathe again only once I was outside, and I was already half-way down the road before I realized I had left the salmon behind.

One afternoon I came home from school and as I hung my coat on the stand in the hall I heard someone talking in a loud voice in the living-room. No other voices joined in. It seemed to be a grim monologue. Believing it was a visitor with a not too friendly way of speaking, I opened the door softly and looked in through a chink.

My father and brother were standing in the room on either side of the fireplace. They held their heads at an angle and looked silently at the radio's loudspeakers.

'Who's screaming there like that?' I asked.

'That's Hitler,' said my father. He let me know with a hand signal that I should be quiet.

I listened. It was my first year of German at school and I understood very little. I grasped only the word *Juden*, which the man uttered more and more often and in an increasingly scornful tone, as though he were kicking the word. Upstairs in my room I could still hear the voice. It penetrated throughout the house. It even drowned the shuddering tap at the wash-basin, which I had turned on because I was curious whether I would still be able to hear it.

I put my books out ready, but before I started my homework I went upstairs to the attic and shut the door behind me. Without switching on the light I went to the middle of the attic and stood there. The sound of the voice was fainter but still very audible. I went back to my room and got on with my work. I tried to study my history lesson about the Holy Alliance with my hands over my ears. I had the same feeling of danger as years earlier, when, with the hard earphones of the head-set on, I had heard the first radio broadcast at Mr Kuisters's. The Mexican dog. I pulled my hands harder over my ears as though I unconsciously felt what that voice would bring about.

The Front Path

Because that Keppels boy began to call us names, things changed in the road. My brother didn't let it bother him; he went for him although the boy was almost a head taller. It seemed to make no impression on him in this situation. I was standing in front of the window when he knocked him to the ground on the path in front of his own house.

'They're fighting,' I called to my mother who was busy in the kitchen.

'Who's fighting?'

'Dave and the Keppels boy. Opposite.'

'Now what's going on? That's a good start.' My mother hurried in to the living-room, drying her hands on a grey check kitchen cloth. 'Call him inside immediately.'

But it was no longer necessary, the fight was over. The boys struggled to their feet and my brother crossed the road with huge strides. 'There we are,' he said, 'he's had what was coming to him.' Blood ran down his chin on to this pullover.

My mother took him into the kitchen to wash his face. 'Why do you fight with that boy?' she asked as she held a flannel under the tap. 'Put your head back.'

'He shouldn't shout filthy Jew.' It sounded muffled behind the flannel she pressed to his nose.

'Did he shout that?'

'Not just once but all the time.'

'From now on you'd better go and play somewhere else.' My mother looked anxiously at the traces of blood in the kitchen sink before she washed them away with a strong jet of water.

We had not long since moved from a suburb close to the forest to a narrow back street in the centre where we had taken a house that bordered the town park at the rear, an extensive piece of land running down to a pond in the middle, full of ducks, swans and moorhens, with a curved wooden bridge. It had a café, playground and rose garden, but I never felt as at home there as in the forest, where my mother took us every day in a wooden push-chair.

I did not then understand why we had to move to such a poor road, which looked even more disconsolate because of the immediate proximity of stately trees and immaculate lawns. I heard only later that my father's business had dwindled so much my parents were forced to take a cheaper house.

The coal-merchant Keppels lived diagonally opposite us in a whitewashed house, the only decent one in the road. Some tumbledown sheds on either side were used to store the fuel. In front of the house, which stood a little back from the rest, there was a carefully tiled front path where we played with the Keppels children. We weren't allowed inside. When Maritje, a freckled girl with thin calves, wanted to go and fetch something, she told my sister Bettie and me that we must wait, whereupon she took other children from the neighbourhood in with her. She left the door open and I peeped into the dark hallway, from which there usually came a cooking smell I did not know. 'They're roasting pork again,' Bettie said with a nasty face.

The day after the fight I saw the Keppels boy coming outside with his school bag under his arm. His mother stood in the doorway, her hand on his shoulder. He had a black eye and a plaster on his forehead. He ducked resentfully under the protective hand and walked down the wide front path with his head high, like someone giving the impression of being the conqueror in his own territory. But level with the storehouses, where his mother's view could no longer follow him, he began to drag his feet, and when he turned round shiftily, I thought I detected an expression of pain round his mouth.

We did not play on the Keppelses' front path any more. There was plenty to do in the road. Next to one of the storehouses lived a woman who sat by the window every day who was said to be suffering from cancer. She had a yellow, bloated face and she invariably leant with her bare left arm on the window-sill. It was fat and white and I was convinced the cancer was in that arm because she never moved it. It lay motionless on the window-sill like an object she put out on display there every morning and then sat herself behind it. I did not dare look at her properly but sometimes I couldn't resist it. At those moments she nodded to me in a friendly way, four or five times, as though she had been waiting for it.

Most of all I liked hanging round Jans and Pieta, the greengrocer women who lived at the end of the road in a ramshackle farmhouse and were very generous. I was always given an apple by Pieta, a thin woman in a blue apron, her hair in a greasy bun in the middle of her head. While I ate it, I watched the chickens scratching about round the yard. Pieta kept chasing them with a broom so at least once Jans was obliged to throw open the lower door of the kitchen and totter outside. She was so fat she had difficulty walking, and I never saw her in anything but filthy underclothes. Her bare feet were stuck into slippers that no longer had a recognizable shape and round her belly hung a purse full of coins. As soon as she saw me she slipped me something, a handful of gooseberries or plums, even if I was still eating the apple from Pieta. I said nothing about these presents at home because if my mother knew I ate unwashed fruit she would have been much alarmed.

Near the entrance to the park was the sweet shop of Miss van Zwol and her daughter Ida, a backward girl, the local butt of teasing. She stood next to her mother in a white apron behind the counter and pulled faces at the children who came to buy gumdrops, liquorice shoelaces or marshmallows for a cent. On summer evenings she stationed herself in front of the shop door, her flat feet wide apart, her wet mouth half open, her eyes like swiftly darting currants under her heavy eyebrows. Whenever they jeered at her and threw pebbles, she began to cry. We could hear her hoarse, throaty noises long after her mother had taken her inside.

Gradually Bettie and I began to avoid the road. I no longer know how much it had to do with what happened on the Keppelses' front path. My brother thought it crazy and said we were scared. But we preferred to seek our amusement in the park, on the swings in the playground, by the pond or at the cactus-bed hidden behind a rhododendron hedge. We cautiously felt the spikes that were as sharp as needles. The same old men sat on the bench around the bed every afternoon, residents of a nearby home. If they saw us in the gaps they called 'Girl, can you screw yet?' and then we withdrew to a safe distance to go on watching them. They chuckled, spat out jets of tobacco juice in the sand and showed each other with wooden gestures how we had been caught trying to escape.

After a year or a year and a half my parents could afford a larger house in a new suburb. My father's business problems seemed to have been resolved.

Early on the day of the move the removal van took up the whole width of the road, just in front of the coal-merchant's storehouse, making it impossible for him to load up. He appeared at the hatch on the first floor increasingly often to watch how we were getting on. He dragged sacks to the front and his impatience became so great that he meanwhile hung one on the hoist there and then secured the rope.

The sack dangled a couple of metres above the removal van, the doors of which were eventually closed.

'Now can I or can't I?' we heard the coal-merchant shout.

'You can, Keppels,' called the removal men. They got into the cab in no hurry.

As they drove off, the man in the storehouse gave the rope a hefty tug. And then everything happened at once. Not only did the swinging sack shoot off the hook, but Keppels's furious manoeuvres caused the sacks that he had placed on the outer edge of the hatch to crash down below. Mountains of coal smashed to pieces on the ground, coal-dust blew over the grey tiles on the front path and in an instant a greasy cloud hid the white house in the corner from view.

I watched with my mother at the window until the swirling dust had settled. We saw how the road surface slowly turned black, as though it had snowed soot.

'They make a mess of their own front path,' murmured my mother as we, warily walking on the coal-dust that grated under our feet, left the road and went on our way to the new neighbourhood.

The Screen

It didn't take long for me to know we had to be on our guard against Nellie. 'Watch what you say,' they told me. 'She's absolutely not to be trusted.' I appreciated that on the following Sunday when, shortly before visiting-time, they put a screen round her bed.

Nellie was on the window side, narrow arched windows that looked out on to a garden where the trees were shedding their damp, brown leaves on to the paths and lawns. A rather sad scene, sombre like our accommodation, a former military hospital with mouldy, grey walls and flaking paintwork, which served as an emergency hospital after the Dutch Army disappeared.

It was the first year of the Occupation. The anti-Jewish regulations would be announced just a few months later, so there was still no difference between me and the other patients. In our ward were women with all kinds of what appeared to be non-serious ailments. Nellie and I were the only TB patients, and because our beds were opposite each other at the end, at first I had just once nodded a hallo to her. I didn't have another opportunity because she hid herself stubbornly behind knees drawn up high. Initially I thought she suffered bad moods. I knew about that: months lying in bed, always the same faces round you, always hearing the same jokes, the same complaints; they are a function of the hospital routine, where everything happens like clockwork, from the first temperature of the day to the last. Plenty of occasions to become bad-tempered. But it wasn't that. Nellie hid herself so that no one would have anything to do with her. No one ever said anything to her. They ignored her. They behaved as though she didn't exist.

In my short hospital career I had not come across someone who was so consistently ignored, as much because a screen was round the bed as for other reasons. In the university clinic, where I had been the previous summer on the terrace of a pavilion with a group of TB patients, a young woman who had fallen ill a few months after her marriage had a

screen put round her bed at Sunday visiting-time so she and her
husband could be a little secluded. She was on my left and the screen,
made of white, varnished metal hung with pleated sheets, completely
hid the couple from view. We were all used to this ritual, but for the girl
on my right it seemed to be something that simultaneously annoyed
and excited her. She didn't have many visits, as her family lived in
Limburg, and she always wanted to know exactly who was sitting
round the other beds.

When the time came again she hung out of her bed and started
hissing at me.

'Are they kissing yet?'

'I think so.'

Her narrow, freckled face went red. She leant over further towards
me, beat her hand on my blankets and whispered: 'Can't you see
anything?'

'Through the screen, certainly.'

'You can push it aside. A chink will be enough.'

'I wouldn't dream of it.'

'They won't notice anything, they're so busy. . . .' Her knees now
stuck out over the edge of her bed. She nearly fell out of it. 'Just for a
moment.'

'Lie back and leave them alone. You'll soon be able to say hallo to
him.'

'You can do it easily. Go on!' She wouldn't stop, prodding me in the
shoulder, tugging at my bedclothes.

The screen was indeed right next to my bed. But I wasn't in favour of
spying on the two of them. I didn't begrudge them their privacy. The
rest of the group on the terrace agreed. We certainly could be jealous
sometimes. We would all much rather have been enjoying ourselves
behind a screen with a man. But you had to be properly married to earn
that privilege.

When visiting-time was over the husband, a pale man with a shock of
hair, came out from behind the screen. He straightened his hair, folded
his rubber raincoat carefully over his arm and hesitated before leaving
the terrace as though he didn't know which way to go. He brought the
faltering to an end with an awkward goodbye to us. We watched him as
he wandered slowly along the garden path and we all swung round
when he turned by the gate and raised his hand to his wife, who, thanks

to a speedy rearrangement by two nurses, had become visible again. The Limburg girl, sulkily slumped back on her pillows, pointed and winked in her direction for quite a time. The newly married girl withdrew from the curious looks and questions and pretended to sleep.

Nellie also always lay deeply hidden in her pillows when her visit was over. But we didn't have to ask her about it. We were glad when that lot had left the ward. The same went for the three girls. Although I didn't find their appearance unpleasant. Heavily made up, in garishly coloured dressing-gowns and high-heeled slippers, the tall one, the redhead and the fatty joined us on the Saturday morning of my first week in the hospital.

'There's that rabble again,' said the woman next to me. 'You're seeing something here.'

'Who are they?' I asked.

'Females who have caught VD from the Huns. They're in a separate room at the end of the corridor.'

Meanwhile the girls were standing chatting by various beds, but their advances were not rewarded.

'Stay away from my bed,' shouted one of the patients to the redhead in the floral dressing-gown, who had planted her elbows on the edge of the foot of the bed. Her good hand – the other was bandaged because of an amputated thumb – made a fist at the girl, who immediately copied the gesture and stuck both her fists in the air, with the result that her wide sleeves fell back to her armpits. Another woman, who had been approached by the little fatty wrapped in bright-pink artificial silk, screamed that she was not grateful for her interest. 'And you can keep your paws to yourself. Understood?'

'Everyone is scared to death of them touching the blankets,' said the woman next to me with her hand over her mouth, leaning towards me. 'You could get infected by those sluts!'

'Hey, a new girl!' called the tall one with a black fringe, on discovering me. She wore a virulent green kimono with side-slits that exposed her thin thighs. 'What's your name, sis?'

My neighbour got in before me. 'We don't have to introduce ourselves to you,' she said. 'Push off!' She pointed furiously towards the corridor.

The three didn't take the hostility seriously; on the contrary, they got the giggles. They had to hold on to one another so as not to fall over, and they made for Nellie's bed after they had deliberately touched every other bedstead. She was the only one they could go to. Nellie sat up for the first time. I heard her chatting and laughing for the first time. She took a box of sweets out of her bedside cupboard and the others fell on them immediately. Noisily they ate their way through the box, dropping their crumpled brown wrappers round them. Then they combed Nellie's hair, plumped up her pillows, banged the bed again and looked round to see if there was anyone else they could pester. Because everyone had already had a turn, they stuck their tongues out at the whole ward, shrieking and pushing each other as they clomped towards the door, where they repeated this number once more.

The following day Nellie's family came. As soon as they appeared in the doorway, the talk of the visitors already sitting round the other beds ceased, as though someone had given a signal for them to be quiet. They were three Nazi Party men. The eldest, a tanned fifty-year-old with short grey hair, led the way. He held his cap clutched under his arm like a briefcase. The belt round his waist and over his shoulder gleamed. The boys following him were tall and could have been twins. Both had straw-blond hair combed flat over their heads. The only difference was in the parting: for one it was on the left, for the other it was down the centre. They wore the same outfit as the older man, the same sharp-pressed breeches and high black boots. They also held their caps under their arms.

The three marched through the ward with short, controlled steps, looking straight ahead, their free right arms swinging in time. Behind them followed a woman dressed all in black. Her worried face had deep creases on either side of the mouth that pulled the corners down. With a curved back, arms stiff against her body, as though she wanted to avoid any contact with the beds, she shuffled over the newly polished linoleum. The room stayed silent. Visitors who sat with their backs to the middle did not look round. But the eyes of the patients who were propped upright in their beds by extra pillows followed the procession until it had disappeared behind the screen, after which conversations started up again in subdued tones.

Later on my mother arrived. At first she wasn't bothered about it, but when she was next to me properly she turned round and noticed the screen. 'Is that the most serious patient?' she asked, gesturing behind her.

A cap hung on one of the bars of the screen. Apparently she had not noticed that either. It was a black cap with a shiny peak. The little belt round it had a buckle in the middle. On the cap's raised front there was an orange-and-black triangle with the wolf-trap insignia of the Nazi Party. It hung so that I could see it just above my mother's head. I lay down lower. The cap stayed visible, so I sunk down even further and finally crept under the blanket.

'Are you cold?' said my mother, surprised. The cap disappeared behind her back, but now I could see under the screen thin iron feet with castors and, in between, heels of black boots, one of the woman's feet in a lace-up shoe with bumps on the toecap. My mother turned round again. She sat up with a jerk, pulled her chair closer to me and looked at me, shocked.

'They use a screen for that too,' she whispered. The cap had come into my view again, so now I lay on my side. We began to talk more softly and my mother sat uneasily on her chair, uncomfortable about turning round, as though the Nazis were keeping an eye on us through the screen.

'Perhaps it's better if you don't come on Sundays,' I said. 'You've seen it.'

'Yes, I see it.'

She got up and left, a quarter of an hour before time.

Nellie's visitors did not come out from behind the screen until everyone else had gone. The men marched away as they had arrived, followed at some distance by the shuffling woman. She pushed one of the swing-doors open so far that it stayed ajar. That's how we could hear the boots stamping all the way down the corridor.

The two nurses who had to tidy the ward put chairs back in place, pulled bedspreads straight, shook our pillows out. Only when there was no more to do round the beds did they move the screen. They wheeled it out of the ward. The iron castors squeaked and sounded almost cheerful, as though each wheel had its own pitch.

At Seven O'Clock

'How strange that I never felt it.'

'It came all of a sudden.' She looked past him at the wall, at the old school clock that had let the weather in, brown stains on the lower part of the clock-face. 'I can phone him around seven o'clock this evening.'

Viktor followed her gaze. 'You've still plenty of time. All the same, it seems to me more sensible to stay at home. I'll call the society and say you're ill.'

'I'm not ill.'

'But you're still in pain. I can see.'

'Not like yesterday. I'll go as normal. It's best to put up with it.'

She tidied her papers and put them in a pile. He followed her to the bedroom, where she looked for her toilet things because she would go to an hotel in any case.

The previous day the anaesthetic seemed to wear off shortly before she came home. She had gone to lie on the sofa. Not in bed, because that would have given him the idea she had something serious, and she wanted to avoid that impression.

When he asked why she was lying there, she had immediately reassured him too. 'Oh, it's nothing. I've just had a little lump removed. Beneath my armpit, close to my left breast.'

He was shocked. 'But you never told me. Why not? How long did you have it?'

'Not that long.' She looked up from the magazine she had started leafing through as soon as she had heard the front door close. 'I had it done at once. It seemed best to me.' She waited a second before she said: 'You needn't worry. They're still intact.'

He did not know what to say to that. The shock was still affecting him. He pressed his hands against his thighs, for her a sign that he was suppressing a violent reaction. Otherwise perhaps he would have thrown the magazine on the floor, pulled the rug away and lifted up her arm. Generally it irritated him if there was anything the matter with her, although since they had been married all she had had was flu a couple of times. He certainly let his anger show when she stayed in bed one day. She may not have been ill, but when that happened he didn't think of doing anything for her, fled the house, went into town to eat, late, in the hope that meanwhile she would have recovered a little. But now he devoted the whole of the rest of the day to her, like the time they had got to know each other six years ago, during a sociology congress in Knokke. He bent over backwards and she submitted to his care uncomfortably. For that reason too she left before four-thirty.

Viktor stood at the window to see how she got out from between two cars that were parked too close to her. It cost her extra effort to manoeuvre the large Renault smoothly out with its heavy steering. Don't let anything show, wave and go. The town was left behind her just a quarter of an hour later. She would have to drive fast to be on time. She wanted to phone at seven o'clock precisely. Then she would have forty-five minutes in which to eat. If she could eat.

It began to get a bit darker, but when she dipped her headlights there was still nothing to see on the road. She felt in the space between the seats with her right hand. Bits of paper, a comb, a started tube of peppermints, sticky acid-drop wrappers. She found a packet of chewing-gum on the floor. She took a rectangular strip out, folded it double, put it in her mouth and began to chew fast to suppress a rising feeling of sickness. Although it gave her a fresh taste, the perception that she had rubber between her molars rapidly gained the upper hand. She wound the window down and threw the little ball out. As usual it stuck to the side of the door. Because she watched it too long, the car began to lurch, which caused the car behind to flash its lights at her. She swerved and at that moment felt a violent pain under her left armpit. Carefully she drew her arm in against her body; the dressing was like a thick wad. She let the arm rest in her lap and reduced her speed.

Perhaps it would have been better to let Viktor phone. He had already dialled the area code when she said that he needn't. She couldn't face the evening and everything it involved, the lectern with the microphone she had to tap to make sure it was working, the carafe of water and glass, weak coffee in the break, the coughing in the hall, thanks from the chairman, who would once more briefly summarize her 'fascinating argument'. Would he call her Mrs Van Stein again when she was just plain Stein? She shouldn't think about it. But she didn't want to stay at home. She already found it unpleasant enough to have to tell Viktor. His concern disturbed her more than it did her good. Could it not still mean nothing? You musn't instantly think the worst. Naturally it appeared to begin like that. But a lump didn't have to be cancer even if it were right next to your breast.

The traffic-lights at a junction went red. She stopped. A Mercedes was next to her. The man behind the wheel still had his sun-glasses on. He looked over to her side. The darker patches of his glasses and the wide black moustache gave his face exaggerated accents as though he had been taken in hand by a make-up artist. With his deerskin driving gloves and scarf loosely round his neck he could have been got up for a television commercial. She would try to get in front of him; she changed into first, her left hand on the wheel. The car moved off fast, just as she intended. In her mirror she saw the man in the Mercedes lean his head forward. He was catching up, he passed her at high speed, then drove in front of her, not a great distance ahead. It wouldn't be all that hard to overtake him again now, but she no longer felt like it. Driving casually she leant back.

He asked where it was. She raised her left arm, put her hand on the back of her head and pointed with her other hand to the spot under her armpit. The doctor had deep-set eyes. His hands were narrow with long fingers, the little finger almost as big as the ring finger. They felt cold. He said nothing and his facial expression didn't change while he examined her breasts as though he wanted to estimate their weight and did not see that they were a good shape. They were in a small room, where instruments were carefully arranged on a table by the wall. It looked like a display. Only the price-tags were missing. Her arm, still raised, was becoming heavy. It was a position she would otherwise have held easily, or with growing excitement, one breast raised, the other straight. She began to perspire. Her skin prickled from the neck to the waist and she had trouble keeping still. She saw a small rust-brown spot on the lapel of his white coat. Blood? Iodine? It hadn't come out in the wash.

After she had dressed, he asked her to accompany him. An appointment had to be made. 'I'll remove it this week and send it off for analysis,' he said.

They walked along a narrow corridor to another room. Three nurses sat at a table with a red-and-white check cloth on which there was a box of chocolates. The lid had a coloured reproduction on it: a still life with tulips. One of the nurses opened the box and offered it to the doctor.

'Someone's birthday?' he asked.

'It was, doctor,' said the eldest of the three.

'Congratulations, then.' He chose a white chocolate with a hazelnut on top, put it in his mouth and wiped his fingers in the palm of his other hand.

'Would you like one too?' The box came in her direction.

She shook her head. 'No thank you.'

'For the figure?' The doctor laughed. It was a superfluous question because he could see she didn't have to worry about her figure.

The nurse closed the box. She wore glasses with tortoise-shell frames. There were little pimples round her nostrils. She tapped the lid with the flat of her hand and took a desk diary with a brown cover out of the cupboard behind her.

'Could you do Thursday at eleven o'clock?'

'That's fine, yes. Thursday.'

At that moment it wouldn't have made any difference if he had said this evening. The atmosphere of the hospital oppressed her as usual, the smell of disinfectant got into her breath. As soon as she smelt that she had the feeling she could no longer be herself. They did things to you to which you had no resistance. You let it happen even though you did not know the outcome. As soon as she got outside, it struck her that she had to go by car to give a lecture the day after.

It was now almost dark. In the distance the rear lights of the Mercedes were getting smaller all the time. He had seemingly given up letting her overtake him again. There was less traffic on the dual carriageway she turned on to and she could use full headlights some of the time. In the beams a truck appeared at the side of the road. It had four stop lights. The upper two were so high it looked like two cars on top of each other. Such colossal freight lorries usually came from Germany. If it's Dutch, there's nothing wrong with me, she thought. At that moment she saw the white number-plate with black numbers. A German.

It could just as well be benign. Otherwise she would definitely have noticed something. But it is also often true that you can already have cancer for some time without knowing it. And then they amputate, to prevent it spreading. First one breast. Don't lots of women walk about with only one breast? There are special bras available with prostheses. Left or right, madam? Or both? Left only. Look here. We have a large selection of models. With or without lace? And what colour had you in mind? There's black too. Only not transparent, naturally. Go to the changing-room. Generally there are tall mirrors with adjustable side-mirrors in which you can spot the shop assistant who has been waiting behind the curtain. Just when you have got out of your pullover and bra she comes in to hand you the newest models and to help you close the clasp. Would you bend forward a little, madam, then they lie better in the cups. May I? And then she puts her hand in and lifts them up. You see? That makes a difference.

She felt hot and turned the heater off. To turn the knob she had to steer with her left hand again. It was difficult. The wound pulled. When she had discovered the lump she walked round with it for a few days before she went to the doctor. When she was in bed she wanted constantly to show it to Viktor. 'Feel here.' But she kept it to herself. He would think she meant something else. His hands would pass over it, playing there, as usual. At times she held her breath because she thought he looked at her longer and differently. 'What do you see?' She said it before she realized it. But he didn't hear.

She remembered the first time. Eleven years old, she was. She raced down the forest path and stopped, silent, panting, behind thick bushes. She heard the others shouting in the distance. 'They'll never find us here,' she said as she hid deeper between the leaves.

The boy followed her and stood close to her. 'Take your blouse off,' he said. His voice sounded husky. His forehead was shiny where damp tendrils stuck to it. There were red spots at the corner of his mouth.

'Why now?'

'I want to look at them.'

She undid the buttons and let the blouse fall from her shoulders. A branch poked into her back. She felt a pressure on her stomach and a warmth inside that went down into her legs. The boy looked like a bird, with his head inclined towards her. She smelt his sweat. 'Wow!' he cried. 'You've got terrific ones!' He stuck his hands out and pushed her breasts, pinched them, turned round and ran away. She took a step back, stayed like that between the leaves which scratched against the upper part of her body before she buttoned up her blouse again. She went into the forest along another path.

'It is high time you were wearing a bra,' said her mother not long afterwards. She took her to a shop where a woman in a black dress assumed with feigned tact that naturally the smallest size was required.

'But have a look at her,' her mother said. She had gone to sit down to be comfortable, one arm on the counter, which was entirely taken up with two loads of white and salmon-coloured cloth. She had to open her coat and the saleswoman went over and under her breasts with her hands. 'You're right,' she said. 'She's already doing nicely. That's certainly a B-cup.'

Nor could she wear pullovers. It was always loose-fitting blouses or dresses that the dressmaker made for her. 'Above all, not too tight at the top because it shows so,' she could hear her mother say. The dressmaker nodded understandingly, with a mouth full of pins, and unpicked the bust seams.

Once again she had to turn in to a side-road, narrower, lined with tall trees that stretched up into the beams of light as though they were attracted to it and leant out one by one. She saw herself in the car: right hand on the wheel, one foot on the accelerator, the other alert, next to it. White posts with red reflectors shot past. Houses where cold light from fluorescent tubes burned. A man with grey hair eating at a table with a bare bulb above it, one elbow by his plate. A brown painting hung on the wall behind him. Crossing a bridge and bouncing up and down with it. Triangles with deer pass and never is a deer encountered. Stop for a closed level crossing. The train rattles by. Go on. Try to keep your eyes closed for one second. Two seconds. Or open your mouth and sing at the top of your voice *Everybody loves somebody sometimes*. She was shocked by her own voice and stopped the song in the middle. On the road in front of her something moved. It was black. It turned grey-brown. She looked into the dazzled eyes of a hare, saw in a flash its translucent pink ears. A light tap on the underside of the car. She shivered and put the heating on half. Just in time she found the signpost. She had to take the first road to the right. She changed down, thought that her dressing moved, but when she felt below her armpit it seemed to be in place.

'It'll be sore for a couple of days,' said the doctor as he stuck the last plaster over her dressing. Before she went to the entrance she had looked round. No one noticed she was going into the cancer institute. A nurse pushed a wheelchair out. In it was an old woman with a flat hat that had dropped over her forehead. Her thin legs in black stockings hung out under her skirt. The nurse pushed the chair so carelessly over the step that the old woman twice lurched out and back. In the waiting-room one or two people were reading. They did not look up as she came in. They accepted it just like that: we've all got the same thing. But mine's yet to be cured!

She chose a place by the window, saw the nurse with the wheelchair cross the road from behind a car, forcing a motor bike to swerve sharply to the left and a delivery van to make an emergency stop. Undeterred, she jerked the chair forwards as though it had a sack of potatoes in it. At the kerb she pulled the chair up with a tug so that the old woman slid back and her legs went up in the air.

The nurse with the tortoise-shell glasses came to get her. 'Will you come with me, Mrs Stein?' she said from the doorway in the lively voice of a tour guide suggesting a new attraction in prospect. She brought her to a room where there was a stretcher-table in the middle and wanted to shave her armpit. But it wasn't necessary. 'It looks neat and tidy,' she confirmed, satisfied.

She had shaved her armpits before she had bought a low-cut dress in a boutique. She couldn't wear anything underneath it. 'You're better off without,' said the girl who was helping her. She undid her bra. 'What did I tell you? I can make the angle deeper for you if you like it like that. You've really got the figure for it. It's no trouble.' With her cold fingers she pulled some threads out of the centre seam and held the material inside. 'Look how good it is on you.'

She lay on a table with a strap around her middle, her arm raised. There was a grey mark on the ceiling close to the lamp hook shaped like a lion's head. The lion's head spread out and became a head with a pointed hat, a man with a beard. Clouds came over, continuously changing their shape. All at once she could smell the sweet scent of the mattress airing in the garden over two chairs, which she lay on if she came home during the day and looked at the sky with the swift clouds, until it was almost too late to go back to school.

The nurse helped the doctor put a rubber apron on over his white coat. Then she put bowls and pots on the glass shelf of a trolley she wheeled to the left-hand side of the table. The skin below her armpit was cleaned with alcohol and the doctor gave her two injections. She felt the place go numb and before she knew it he was busy with his scalpel. The nurse stood on the other side and assisted him, leaning over her, so she could not see what was happening. She could not follow what was going on in the edge of the metal lamp either, because the light dazzled her. She just heard the clicking of metal instruments. It was as though she was involved with something on the table, which she did not have to do anything about and from which they deliberately excluded her. Now and then she could feel she was being touched, but it could have been by accident.

'This is it.' With tweezers the doctor held up something that looked like a piece of yellow fat, chicken fat that she always cut away from the skin before she roasted the chicken. She had thought it would be round, that it would look like a little marble – it had felt like that too – and that it would have been another colour, pink or brown. She didn't know why. He let it fall into a dish the nurse held up for him at the height of her stomach. The dish was the shape of a rum bon-bon. There was another one on the glass shelf, full of wads of bloody cotton wool. The doctor was already stitching up the wound. He had threaded a curved needle and his hand went regularly up and down. Once or twice he held the thread in a loop, tied a knot and snipped the thread. The girl in the boutique had gone about it the same way. 'I'll tack a thread through,' she said. 'Perhaps I'd prick you with pins, and such a low neck must sit well.' She could follow in the mirror, seeing the needle with the white tacking thread pulled tight after each stitch.

The nurse wheeled the trolley away. The doctor washed his arms and hands and held them under the tap for a long time. As he rolled his shirt-sleeves down and carefully buttoned his cuffs he advised her to take a pain-killer when the anaesthetic wore off.

She asked when she could hear the results of the biopsy.

'It'll take until at least after the weekend.'

'Isn't it looked at immediately?'

'Yes, it is.' He took his jacket from the cupboard, turned round and looked at her, thinking it over, his arm half in the sleeve. 'But then again, before I get the report . . .'

'Can I phone you?'

'Yes, if you wish . . . phone me tomorrow evening at home around seven o'clock.'

It was a quarter to seven when she parked in the market square. Her whole left arm seemed to be numb from the cramped position she had been sitting in for the last hour. As she got out she heard music. On the opposite side of the square a group of people stood round four members of the Salvation Army. A tall boy blew loudly on a trumpet, two girls in bonnets played clarinet and tambourine and an old man beat the big drum. What they played sounded sharp but jaunty. Crossing over towards a café-restaurant, she surprised herself by walking in time to the music. She slowed down and went up the two steps to the entrance. She saw on the clock above the counter that only three minutes had passed since she had arrived. A bored waiter leant against a bar stool looking at the empty room. He came to life only after she had sat down and looked in his direction. She ordered a cold drink and asked where the telephone was. He pointed to a door next to the counter. 'You can use it now,' he said.

She nodded, looked in her bag for the packet of cigarettes before she took her coat off. Her blouse stuck to her but below her back she felt a cold spot, as though there was dead flesh there. She compared the time on her watch with that on the café clock and confirmed the clock was a minute slow. The cold drink, which the waiter had put on a beer-mat by her, tasted of sweetener. Her fingers were clammy, the lighter almost slid out of her hand.

A small white delivery van with the picture of a red lobster on the side stopped in front of the café. *Queen Wilhelmina Foundation for the Campaign against Cancer* was written beneath it in a semicircle. They were playing a foul joke on her and no one would believe her if she told them. Six minutes to go. Two lanky boys sauntered past the window and stared inside. One made a face and stuck his tongue out at her. Behind her in the room the waiter put the television on. A woman in a flowery dress and two children went to sit in front of it. She heard a familiar signature tune, vaguely saw the ridiculous exhortations to buy a washing-powder, a snack and a super-healthy margarine. A mannequin with a large white bra appeared on the screen. It turned round slowly. 'Cross your heart,' called a woman as she followed the diagonal lines of the bra with a hand gesture. After the last advertisement she stood up.

It was oppressive in the telephone booth, a narrow cubicle where the light coming in flickered on and off. She pulled the door firmly shut behind her. As she picked up the receiver and dialled the number, she felt the walls closing in on her. Her diary fell on the floor and she had to begin dialling the area code again. Several numbers had been written on the wall above the telephone. She also saw a drawing of a woman with big round breasts. The nipples were drawn with such force that there were holes in the wall.

The telephone rang three times. 'This is Mrs Stein. I arranged to phone you at seven o'clock.'

'Oh yes. Wait a moment.'

It was silent at the other end. She could hear only some crackles as though the line were faulty. The woman's breasts were larger than the face and she saw no more than the beginning of the legs. The conversation must have been too short to complete the figure. She counted the digits of a number: seven, including three fives. *Van Delden* with a question mark. *Jonkersma 070. Ada Rievers.* Who was Ada Rievers? *I love Jayne Mansfield*, written large next to the telephone. Agitated, she searched the wall for more names, more numbers; feeling pressure all of a sudden in the region of her stomach, she put her hand over the left half of the drawing so that only one breast remained visible. With a wet finger she tried to rub out the left breast. It became a black smudge. Of course he's got to go and look at his papers, or perhaps he was considering how he should tell her. It's only a question of amputation. On one side. You should have no more trouble afterwards. Lucky that you were so prompt about it.

Her ear prickled. It was as though stale air were coming out of the receiver. There were grey flecks round the holes. Dried spit.

'I had to keep you waiting while I looked at the report.' She was shocked by the voice that came through unmistakably. 'It has been analysed and I can reassure you. It was a benign growth.'

'Benign?'

'Yes, completely benign. Come next week during office hours and the stitches can be removed.'

'Yes . . . thank you. . . .'

She pushed the door open and breathed as though she had been under water for too long. Back at her table she got her diary out of her bag and noted down the appointment with the doctor. Might they not have made a mistake at the laboratory? She looked round. The café now appeared quite different. Various tables were occupied, the television was off and the waiter walked to and fro busily with full trays. The delivery van was no longer in front of the door. Had it really been there before?

On the clock above the counter it was five past seven.

Talking of Luck

As I crossed the market-place one Sunday afternoon in my home town, shortly before the outbreak of war, it struck me as unnaturally quiet. I saw no pedestrians, no cyclists, no cars; the square was deserted under a pale sun and there were only a couple of motionless pigeons on the bandstand. The round cobbles of the pavement had a bluish glow and a yellow haze hung over the houses, here and there some windows were open. A slight shimmering of the net curtains was the only movement I could detect. The chairs outside the café next to the market-hall were empty. Even the waiter, who usually stood in the doorway in his white jacket, was missing. It was dark behind the plate-glass windows.

I stayed on the pavement and carefully took a few steps backwards until my heels touched the front of a chemist's shop. There I became aware of an uneasy feeling that something must have happened in the town, which everyone except me knew about. I wondered what I ought to do. Could I walk on normally and break the silence with the sound of my footsteps?

I no longer know how long I stood there; it could have been half a minute, perhaps a few seconds. But when I saw two cyclists coming out of a side-street, slowly pedalling across the Market, at least a quarter of an hour seemed to have gone by.

Three weeks later the Occupation began. I went away, far from the town, and returned only some considerable time after the Liberation. Again I crossed the market-place. The bandstand had had to make way for a car-park, full of cars. The pavement with the round cobbles was unchanged, although white stripes were now painted on them. The grey-blue, lozenge-shaped tiles on the steps were still there; they brought to mind plaques of old, dried-out liquorice. Traffic-lights had been put up and new shops with fronts of steel and glass made the familiar façades almost unrecognizable.

In front of the town hall steps I met a woman who stopped me. 'Don't you know me any more?' she asked. She wore a check coat and had close-cropped brown hair. I seemed to know her but couldn't recall her name. 'We sat together at school.' She put her hand on my arm. 'How are you?'

'Well,' I said.

'You got through the war?'

'As you see.'

'Your brother and sister?'

'No.'

'And your parents?'

'Not them either.'

She looked at me in silence. The smile on her mouth turned into a forced twist. There were dark dots over her upper lip as though she had shaved there, the skin under her eyes was lightly wrinkled.

She bent towards me, her hand still on my arm. 'Then you can count yourself lucky.'

She grinned broadly now, relieved, gave me a little squeeze, and then we took leave of one another.

As I crossed the market-place, navigating my way between cars and cyclists, the picture of that pre-war Sunday afternoon suddenly came to me: the deserted, deathly silent square where all I had seen moving was a net curtain, and it was only then that it became clear to me that it must have been a fearful suspicion which caused me to stand against the front of the chemist's, and the whole atmosphere of resignation had impressed upon me a premonition that something dreadful was going to happen.